BANANA FOX AND THE BOOK-EATING ROBOT

A GRAPHIC NOVEL BY
JAMES KOCHALKA

graphix

An Imprint of
SCHOLASTIC

For Eli and Oliver

Library of Congress Control Number: 2020946437

ISBN 978-1-338-66052-4 (hardcover)
ISBN 978-1-338-66051-7 (paperback)

10 9 8 7 6 5 4 3 2 1   21 22 23 24 25

Printed in China   62
First edition, October 2021

Edited by Megan Peace
Book design by Steve Ponzo
Creative Director: Phil Falco
Publisher: David Saylor

CONTENTS

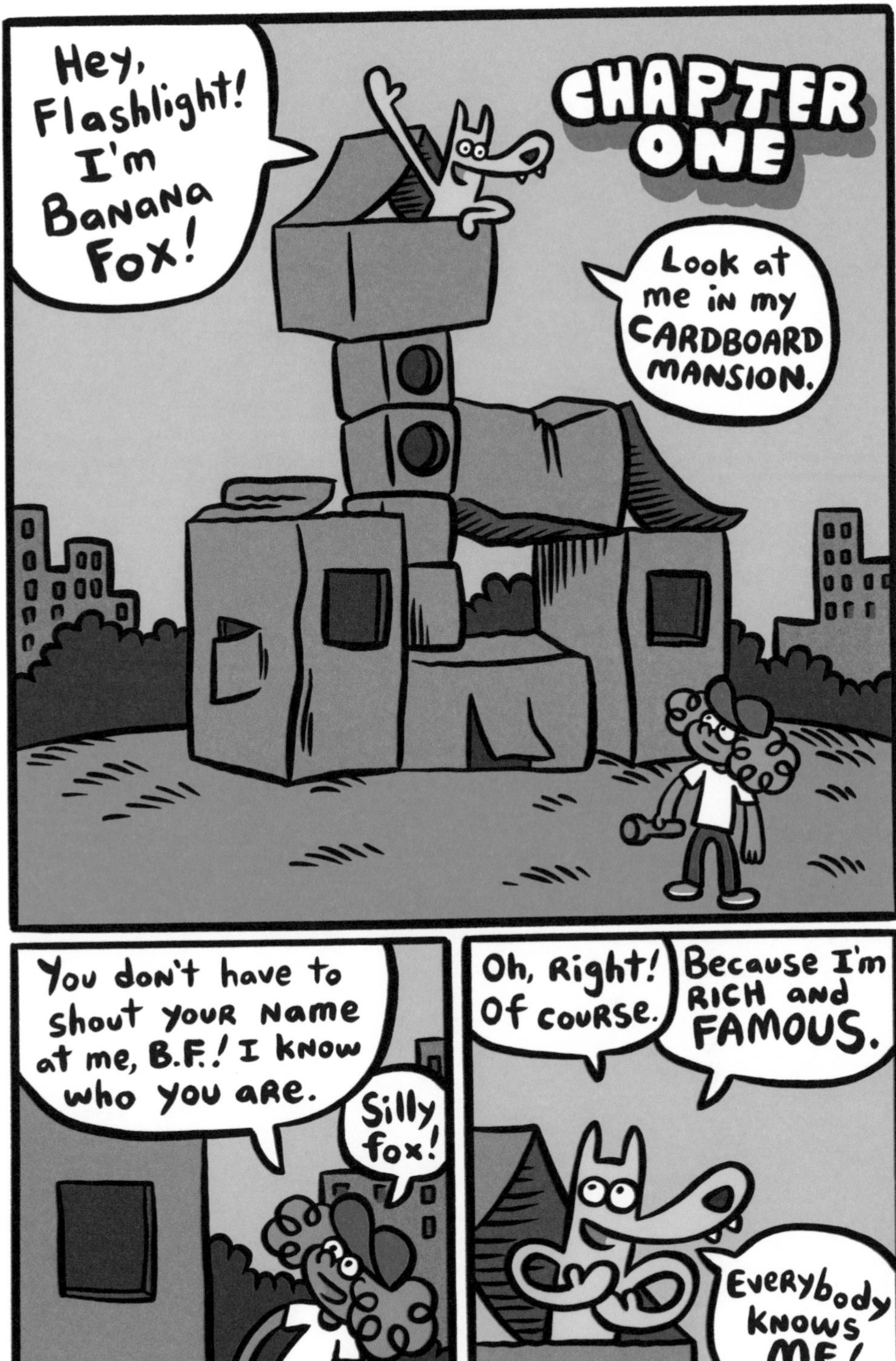
CHAPTER ONE
Hey, Flashlight! I'm Banana Fox!
Look at me in my CARDBOARD MANSION.
You don't have to shout your name at me, B.F.! I know who you are.
Silly fox!
Oh, Right! Of course.
Because I'm RICH and FAMOUS.
Everybody knows ME!

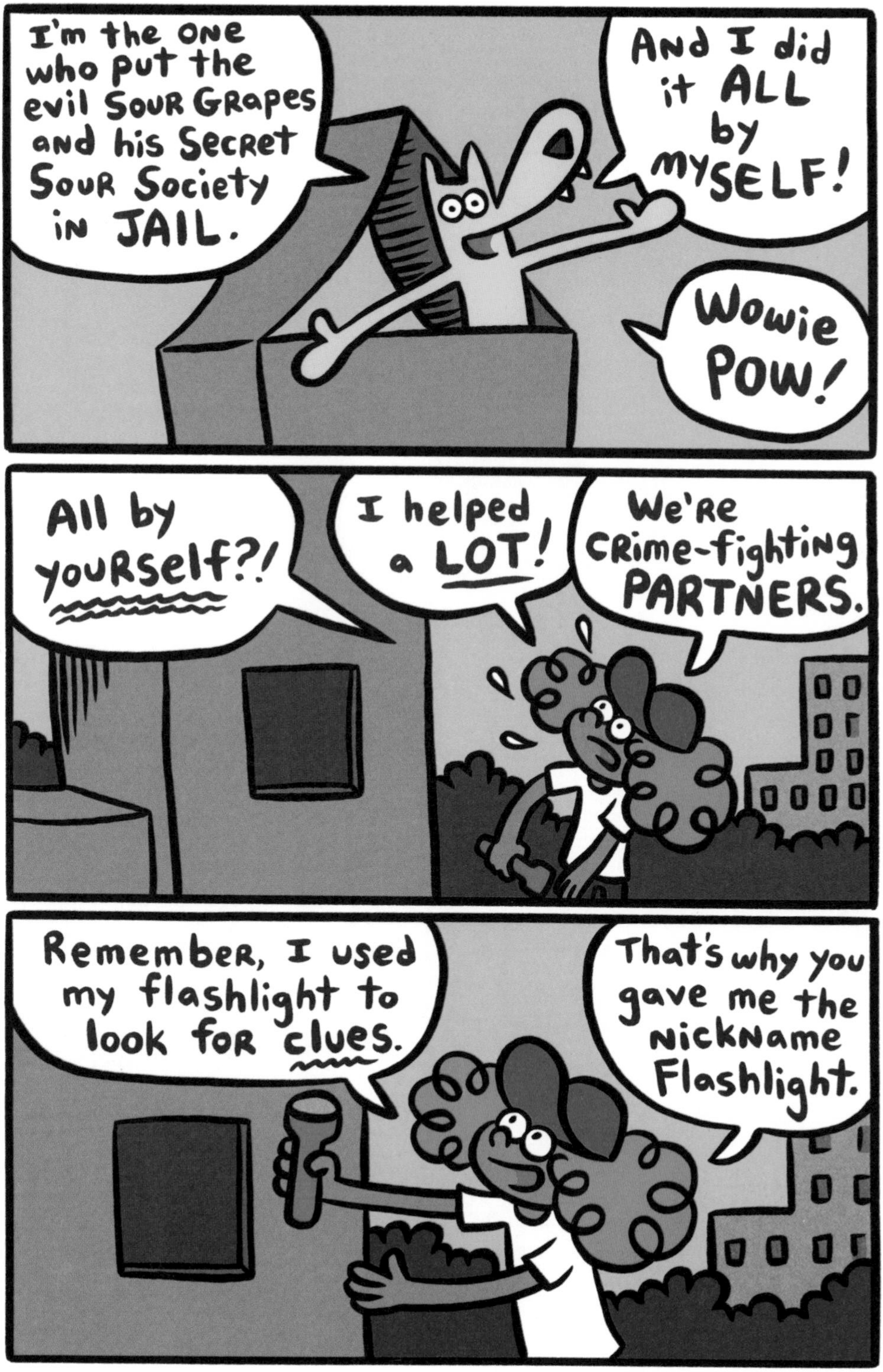
I'm the one who put the evil Sour Grapes and his Secret Sour Society in JAIL.
And I did it ALL by MYSELF!
Wowie POW!
All by yourself?!
I helped a LOT!
We're crime-fighting PARTNERS.
Remember, I used my flashlight to look for clues.
That's why you gave me the nickname Flashlight.

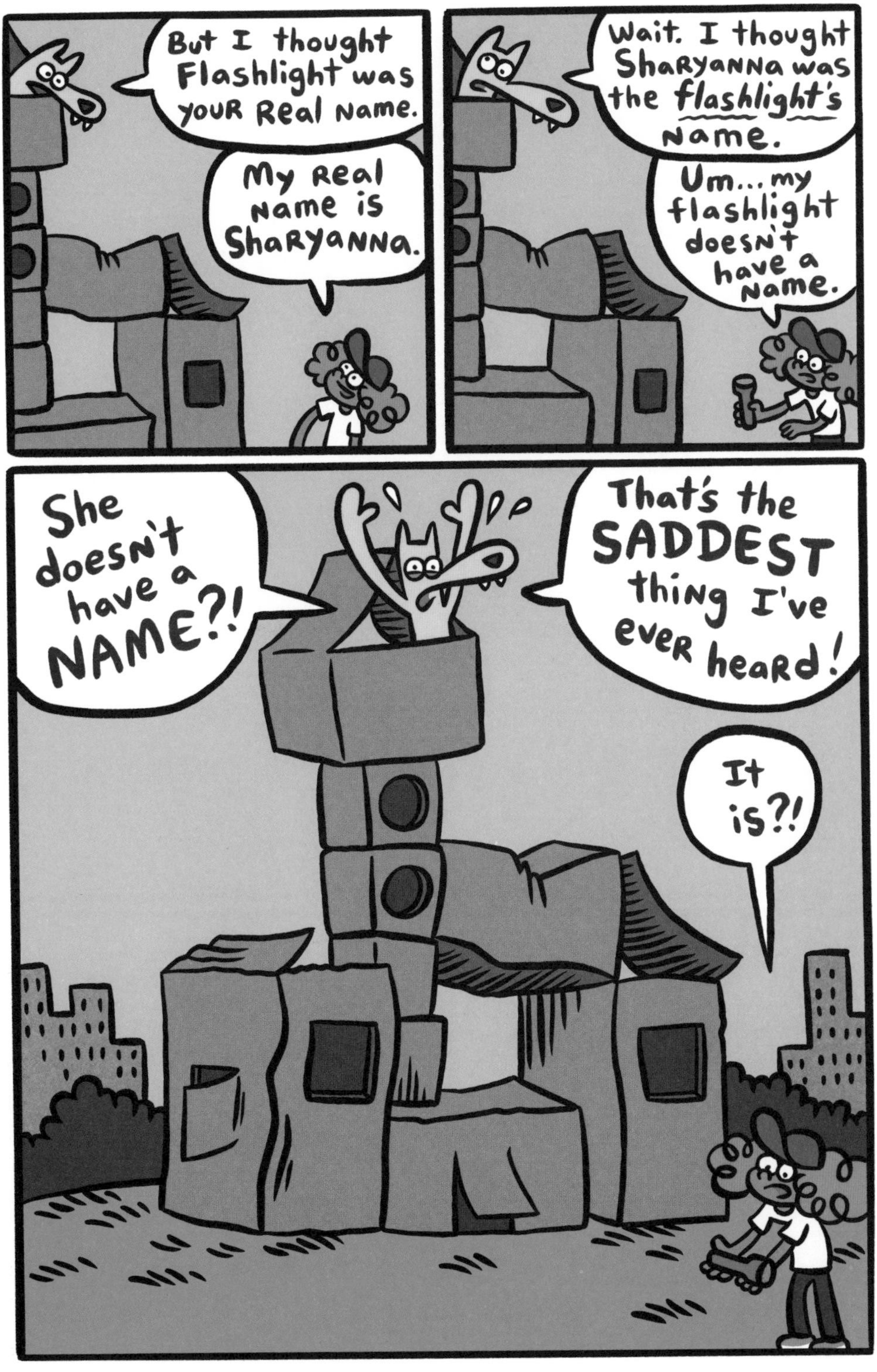
But I thought Flashlight was your Real Name.
My Real name is Sharyanna.
Wait. I thought Sharyanna was the flashlight's name.
Um... my flashlight doesn't have a name.
She doesn't have a NAME?!
That's the SADDEST thing I've ever heard!
It is?!

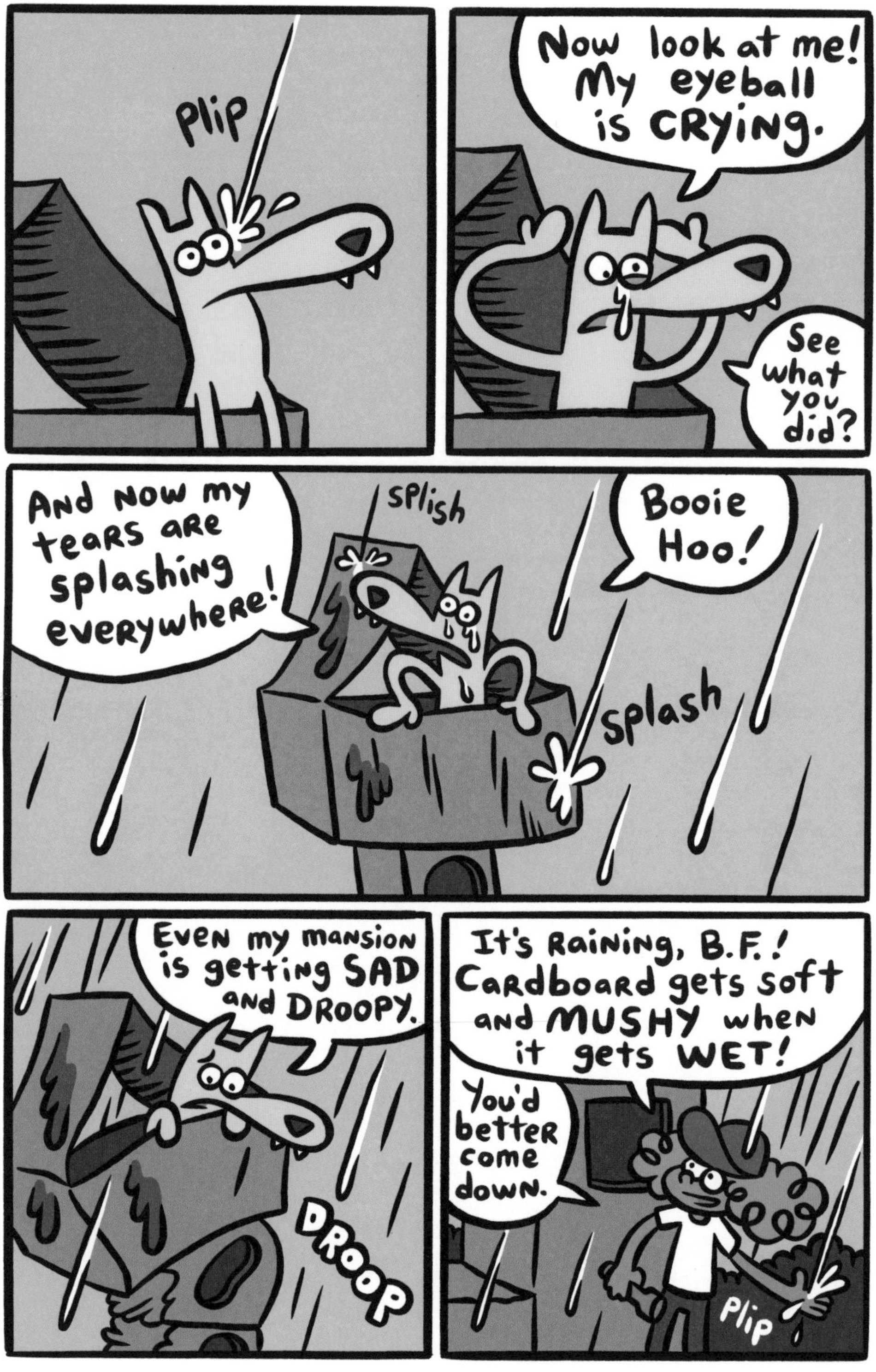
Plip
Now look at me! My eyeball is CRYING.
See what you did?
And now my tears are splashing everywhere!
splish
Booie Hoo!
splash
Even my mansion is getting SAD and DROOPY.
DROOP
It's Raining, B.F.! Cardboard gets soft and MUSHY when it gets WET!
You'd better come down.
Plip

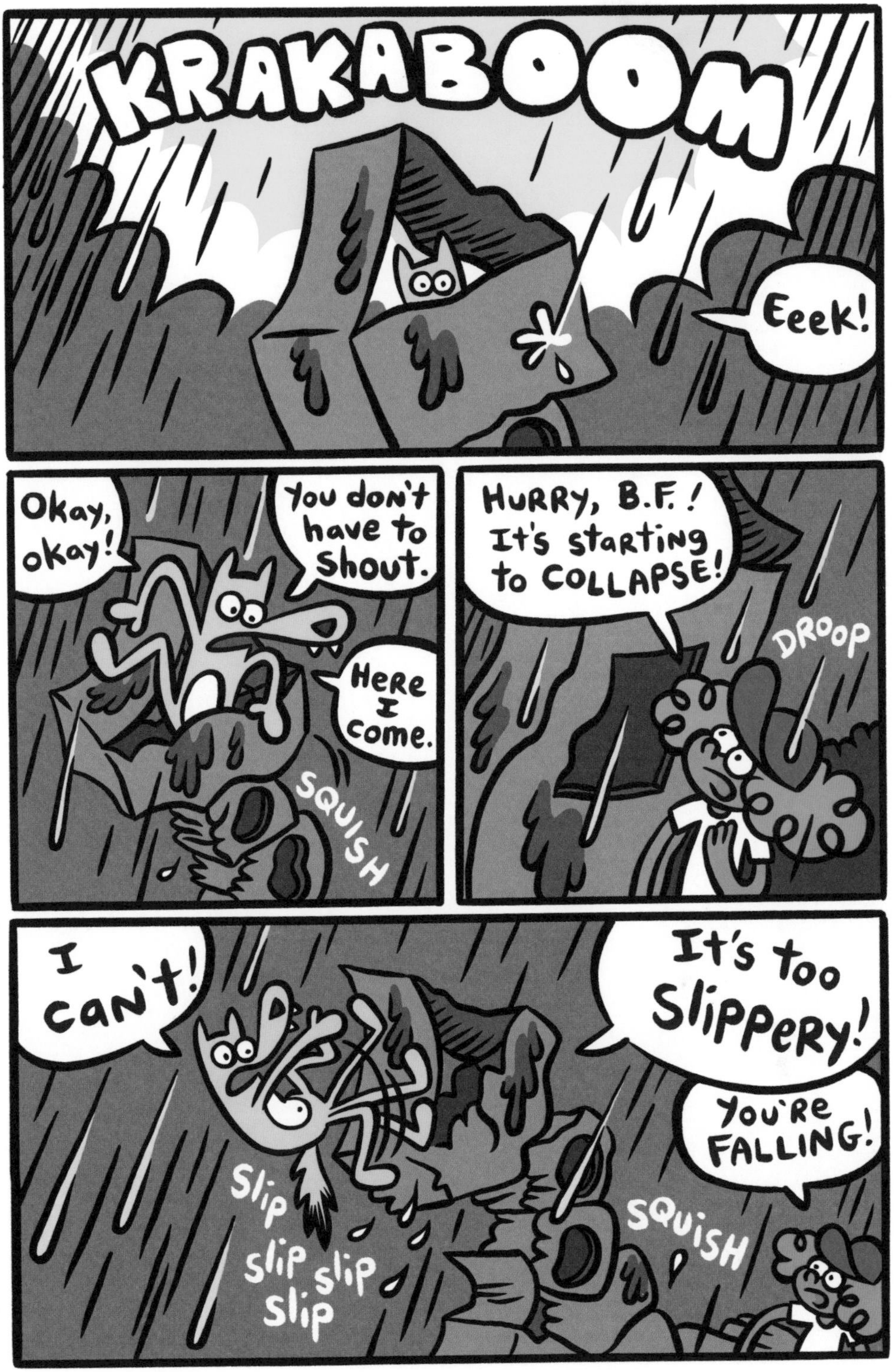
KRAKABOOM
Eeek!
Okay, okay!
You don't have to shout.
Here I come.
SQUISH
HURRY, B.F.! It's starting to COLLAPSE!
DROOP
I can't!
It's too slippery!
You're FALLING!
Slip
slip slip
slip
SQUISH

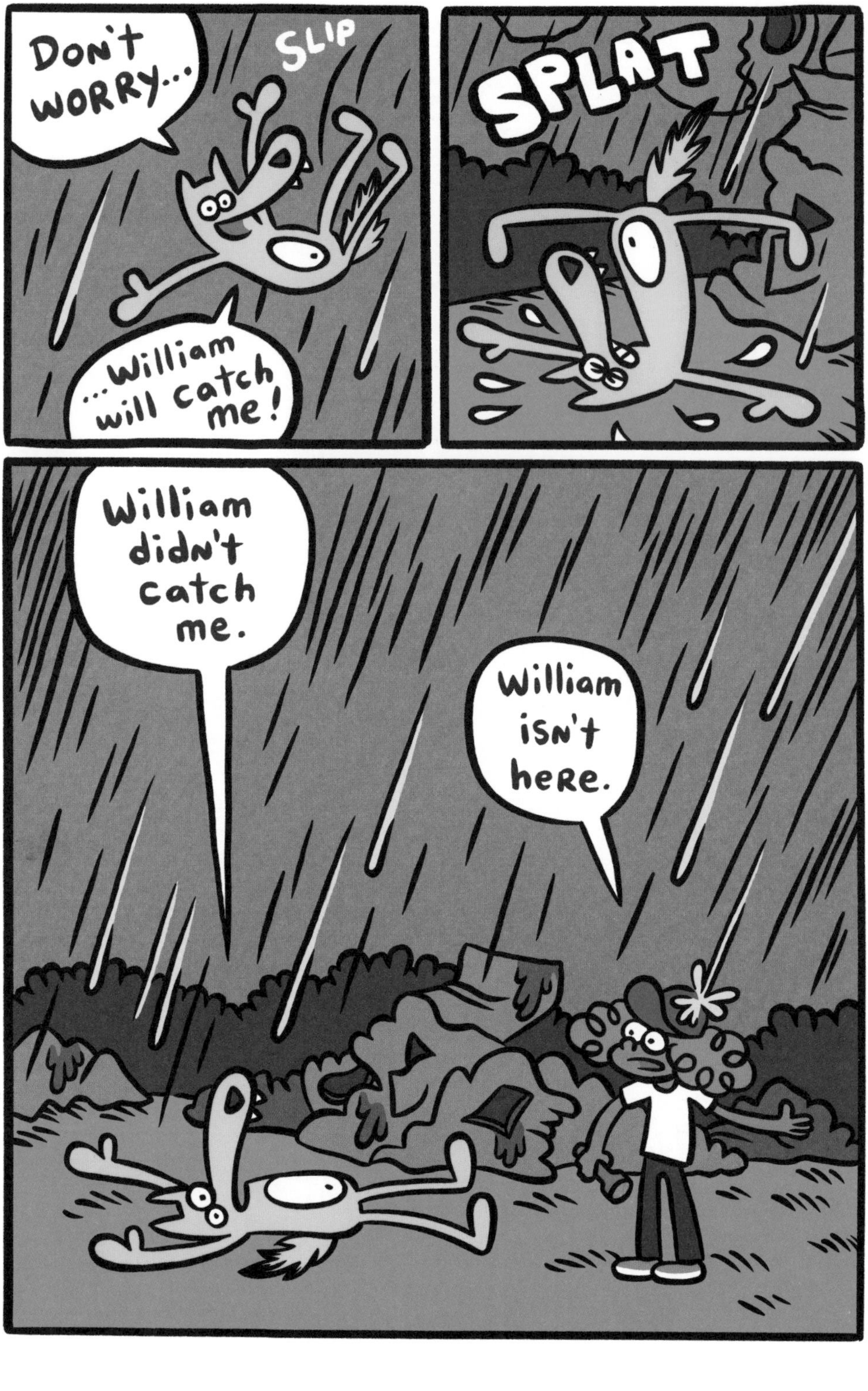

Don't WORRY...
SLIP
...William will catch me!
SPLAT
William didn't catch me.
William isn't here.

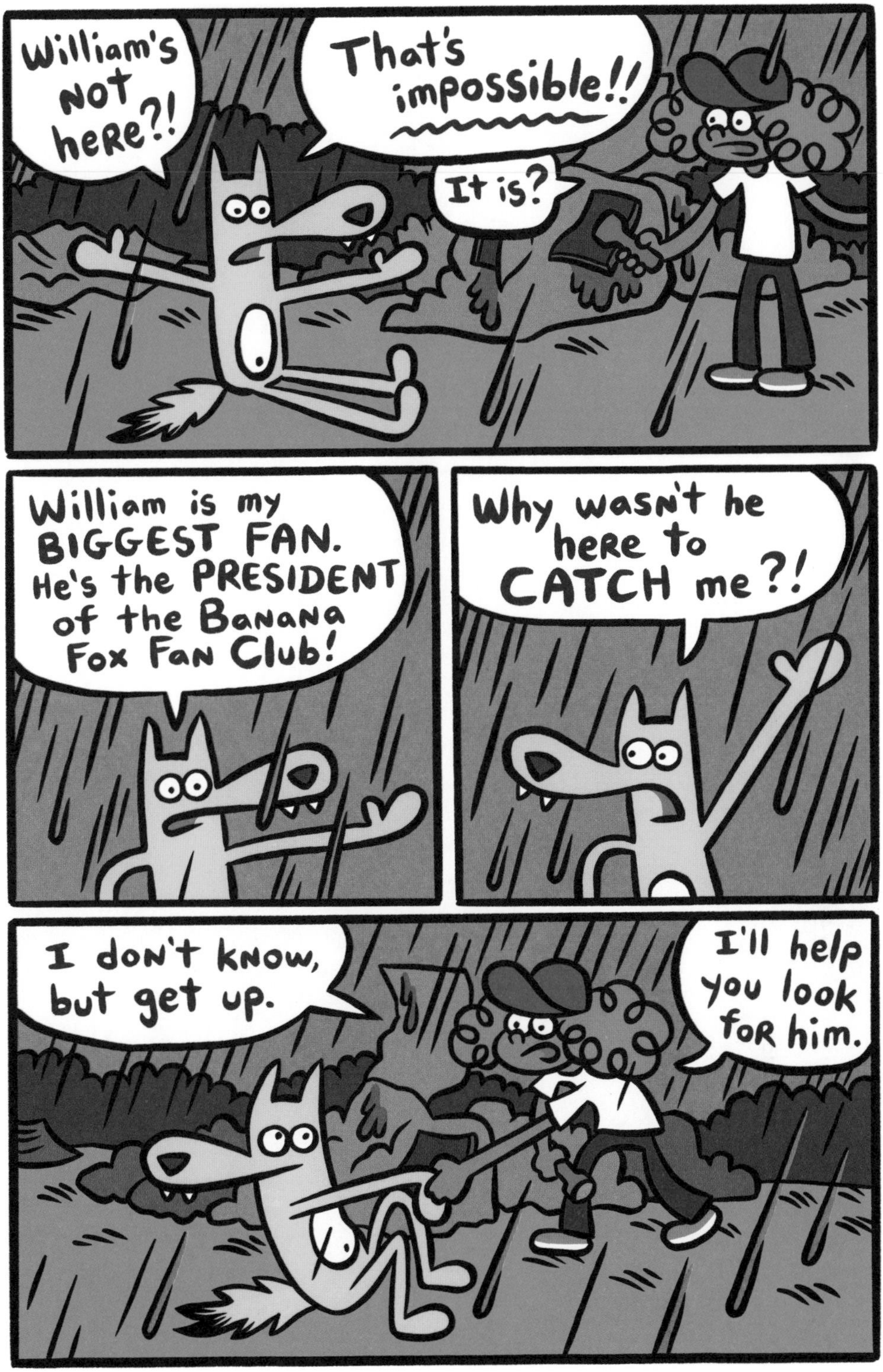
William's not here?!
That's impossible!!
It is?
William is my BIGGEST FAN. He's the PRESIDENT of the Banana Fox Fan Club!
Why wasn't he here to CATCH me?!
I don't know, but get up.
I'll help you look for him.

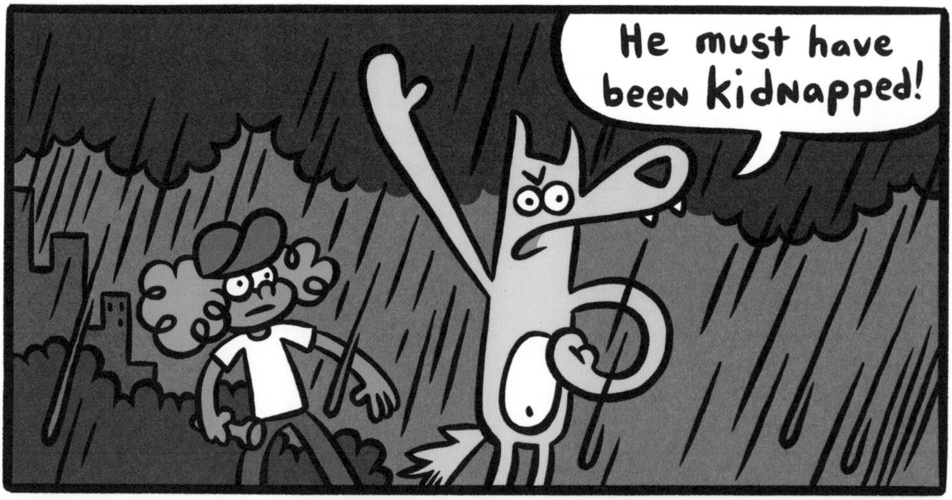
He must have been kidnapped!

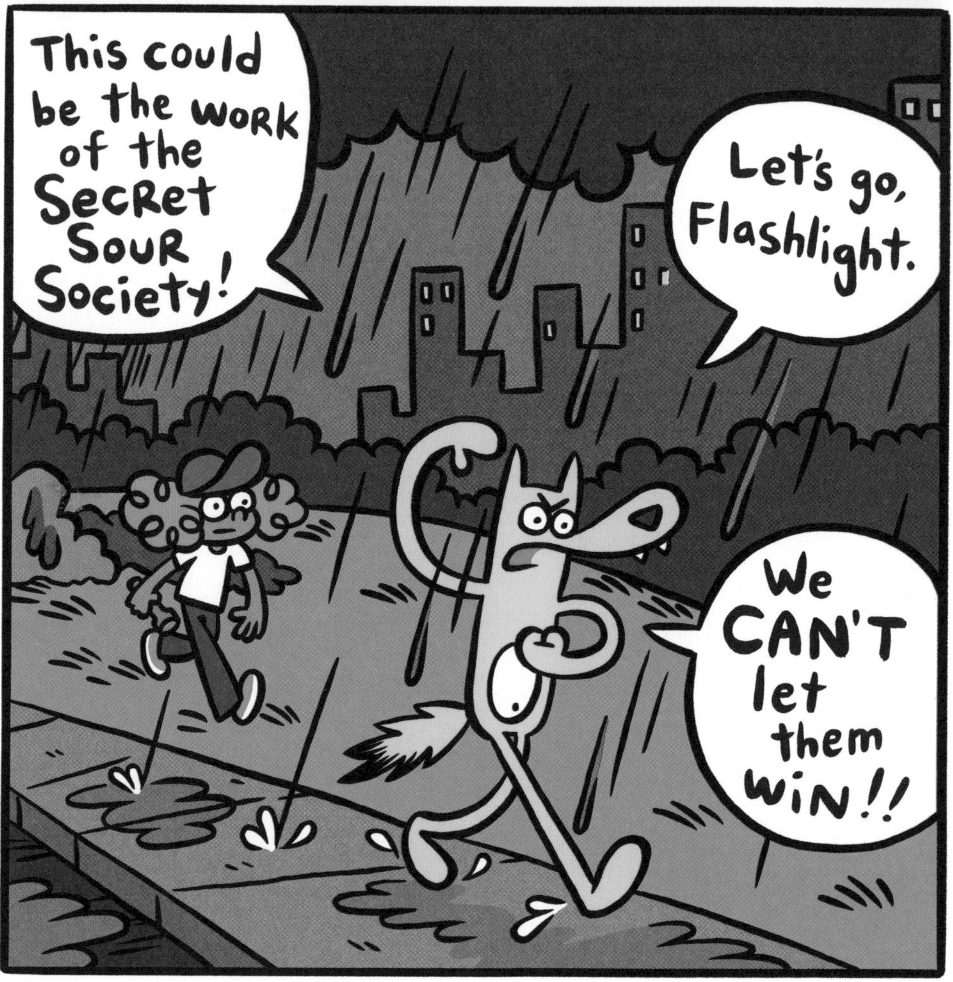
This could be the work of the Secret Sour Society!
Let's go, Flashlight.
We CAN'T let them win!!

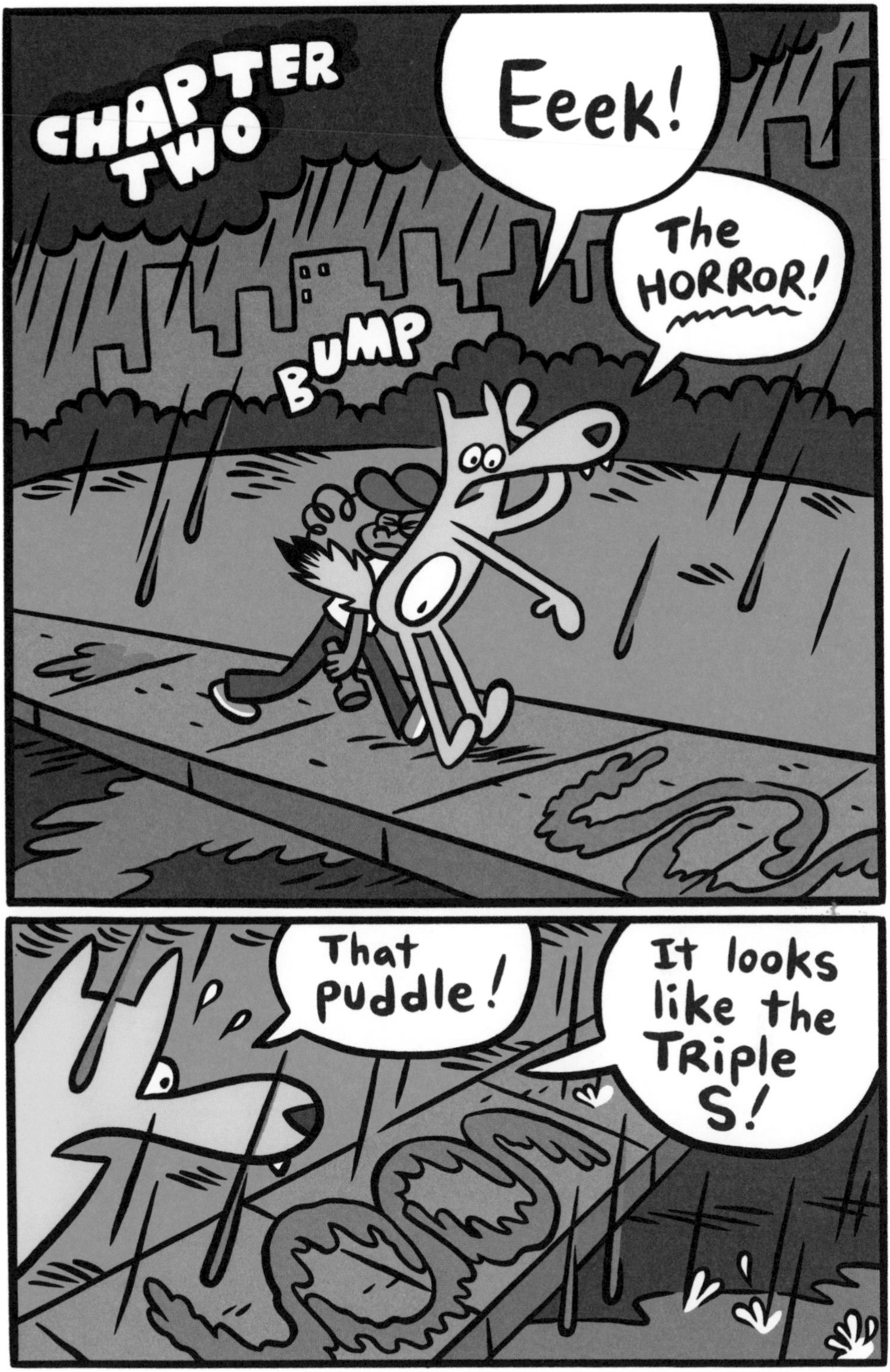
CHAPTER TWO
Eeek!
The HORROR!
BUMP
That puddle!
It looks like the TRIPLE S!

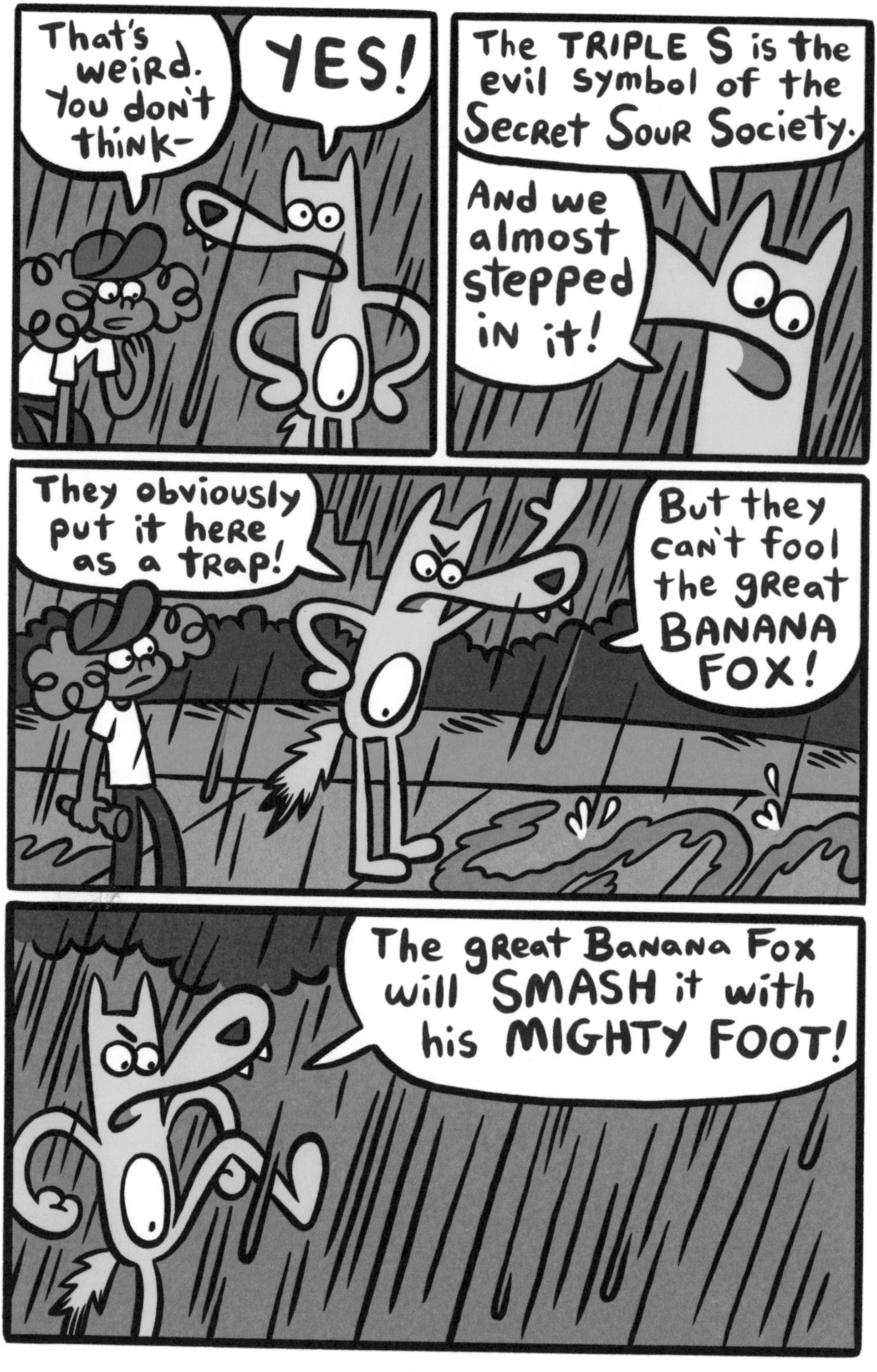
That's weird. You don't think-
YES!
The TRIPLE S is the evil symbol of the Secret Sour Society.
And we almost stepped in it!
They obviously put it here as a trap!
But they can't fool the great BANANA FOX!
The great Banana Fox will SMASH it with his MIGHTY FOOT!

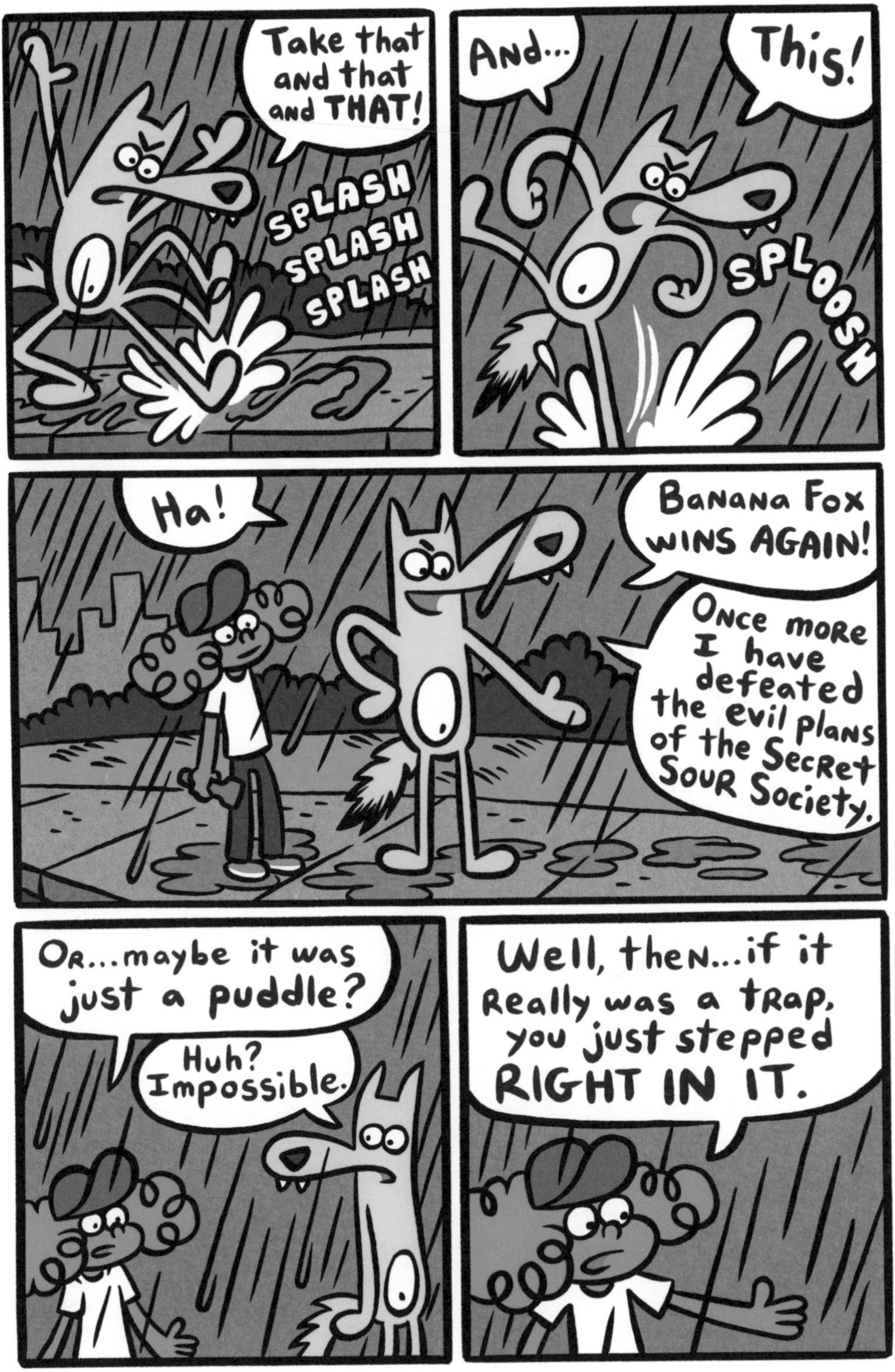
Take that and that and THAT!
SPLASH SPLASH SPLASH
And...
This!
SPLOOSH
Ha!
Banana Fox WINS AGAIN!
Once more I have defeated the evil plans of the Secret Sour Society.
Or...maybe it was just a puddle?
Huh? Impossible.
Well, then...if it really was a trap, you just stepped RIGHT IN IT.

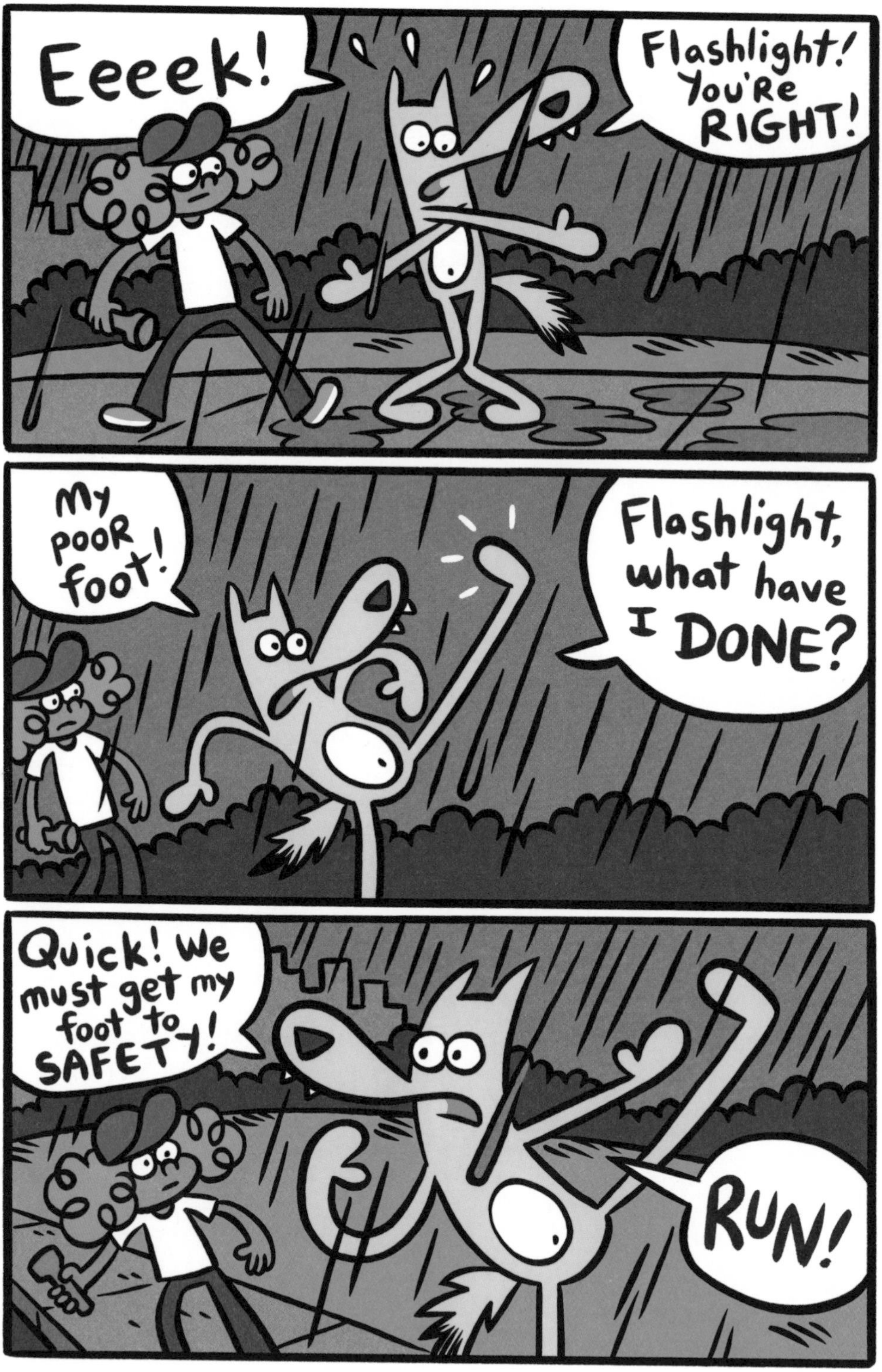
Eeeek!
Flashlight! You're RIGHT!
My poor foot!
Flashlight, what have I DONE?
Quick! We must get my foot to SAFETY!
RUN!

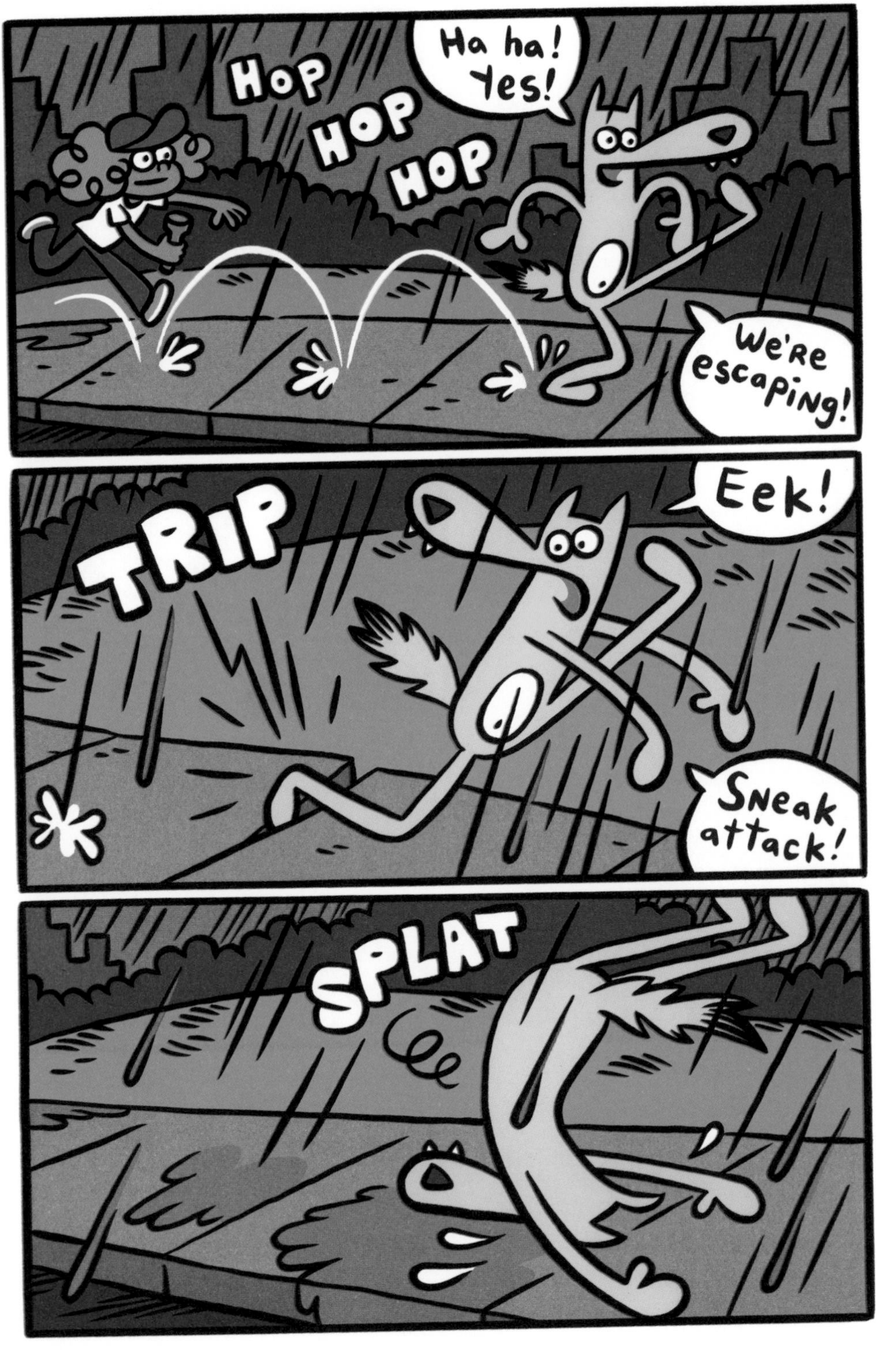
Ha ha! Yes!
HOP
HOP
HOP
We're escaping!
Eek!
TRIP
Sneak attack!
SPLAT

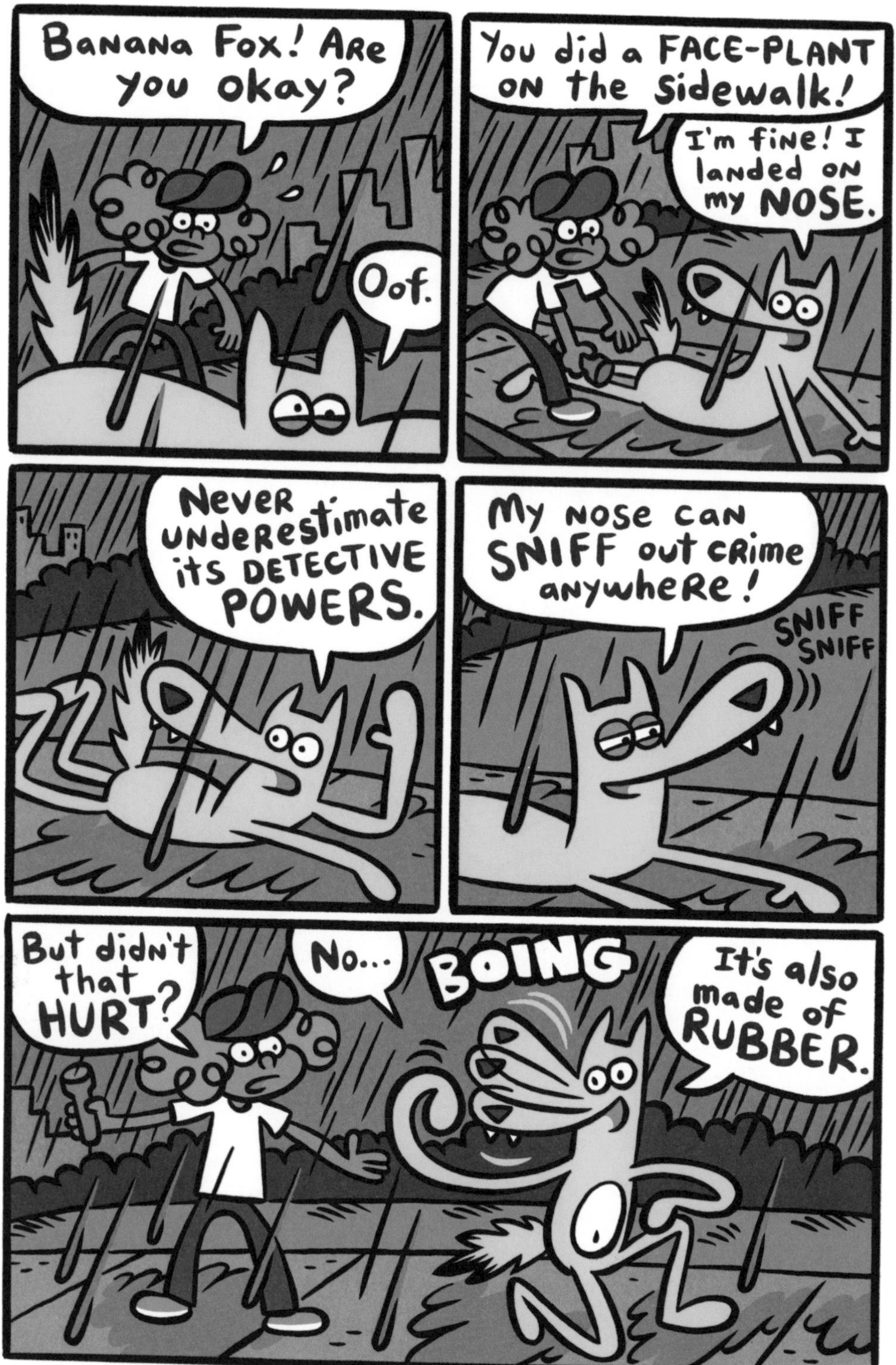
Banana Fox! Are you okay?
Oof.
You did a FACE-PLANT on the sidewalk!
I'm fine! I landed on my NOSE.
Never underestimate its DETECTIVE POWERS.
My nose can SNIFF out crime anywhere!
SNIFF SNIFF
But didn't that HURT?
No...
BOING
It's also made of RUBBER.

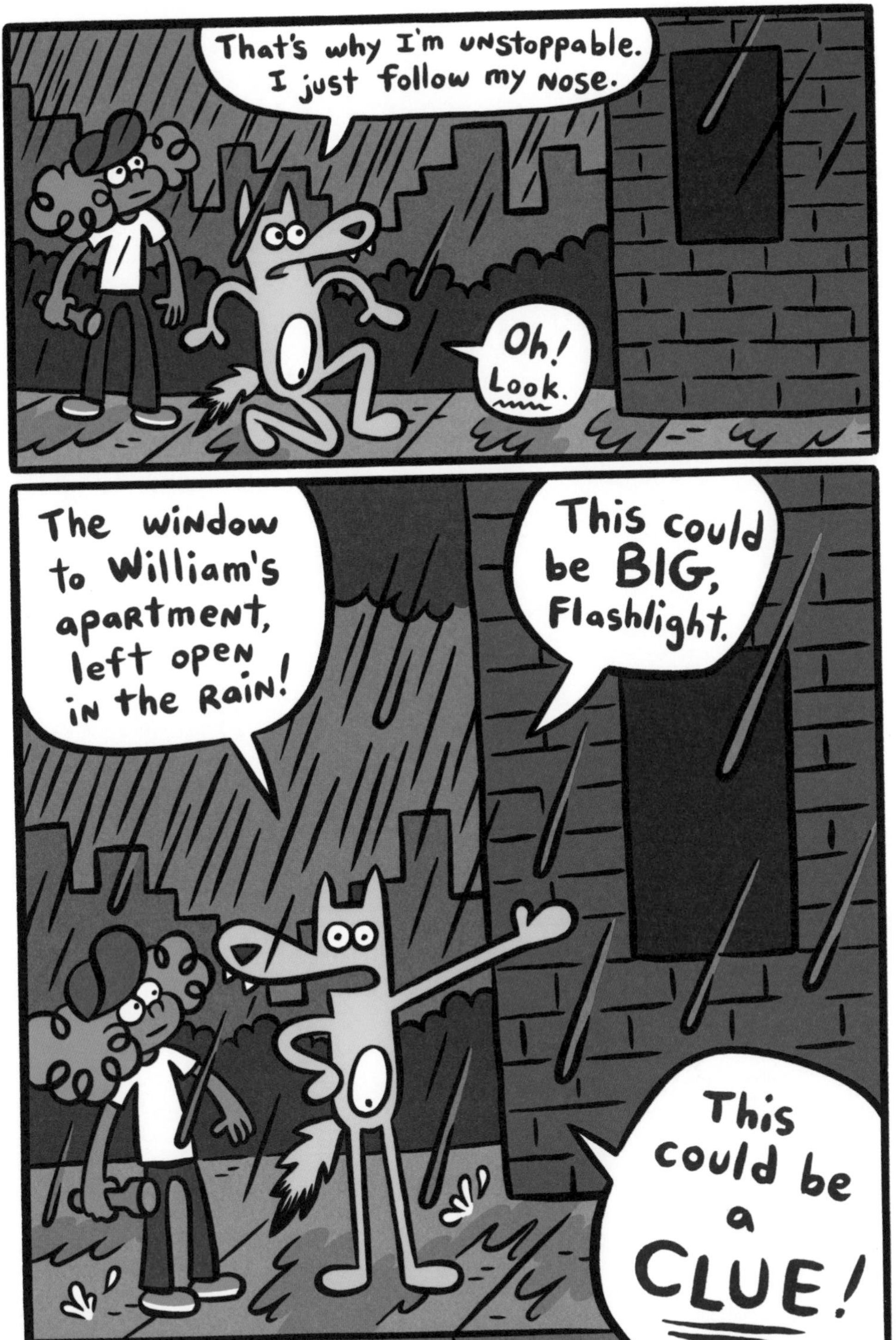
That's why I'm unstoppable. I just follow my nose.
Oh! Look.
The window to William's apartment, left open in the rain!
This could be BIG, Flashlight.
This could be a CLUE!

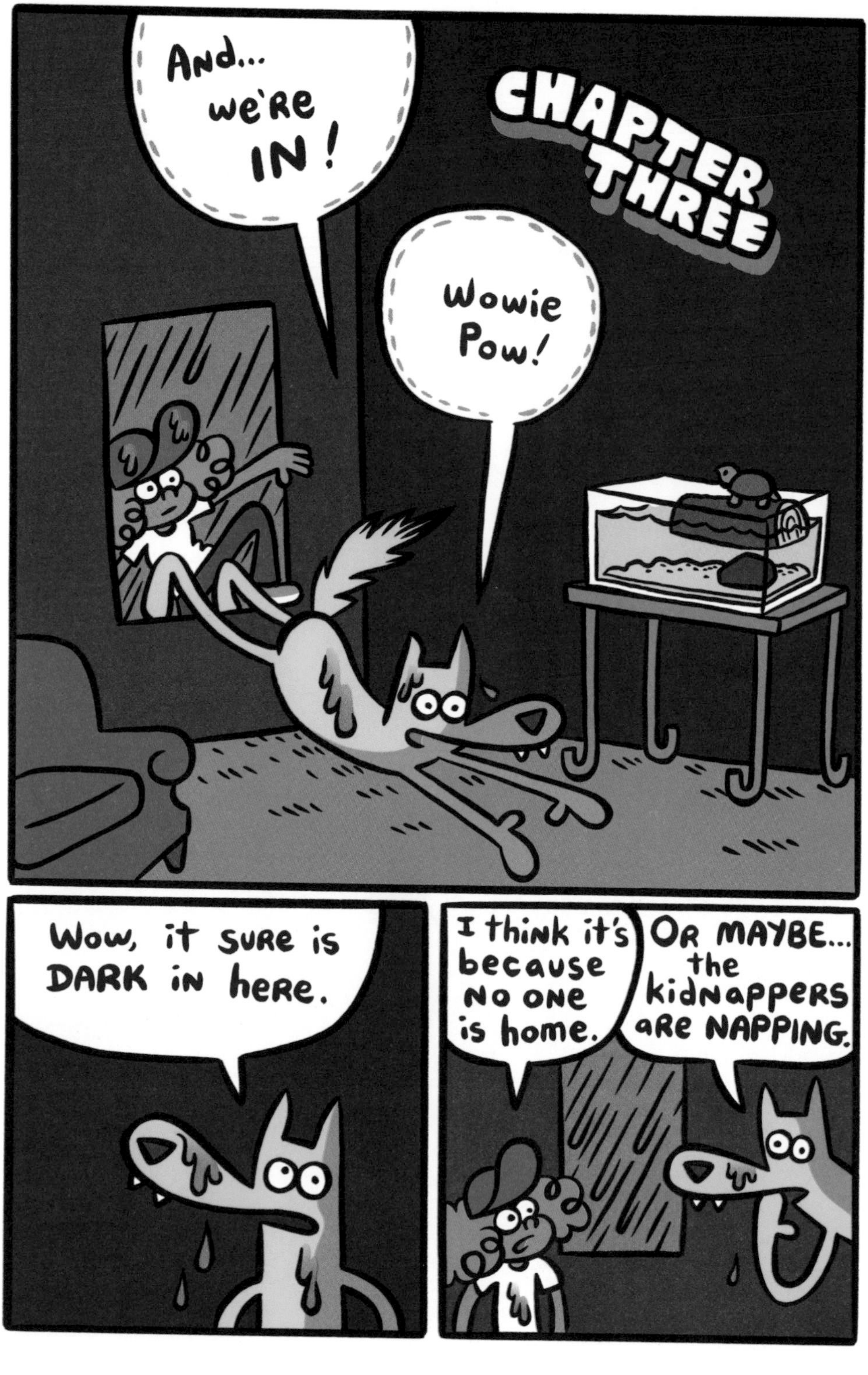
And... we're IN!
CHAPTER THREE
Wowie Pow!
Wow, it sure is DARK in here.
I think it's because no one is home.
OR MAYBE... the kidnappers are NAPPING.

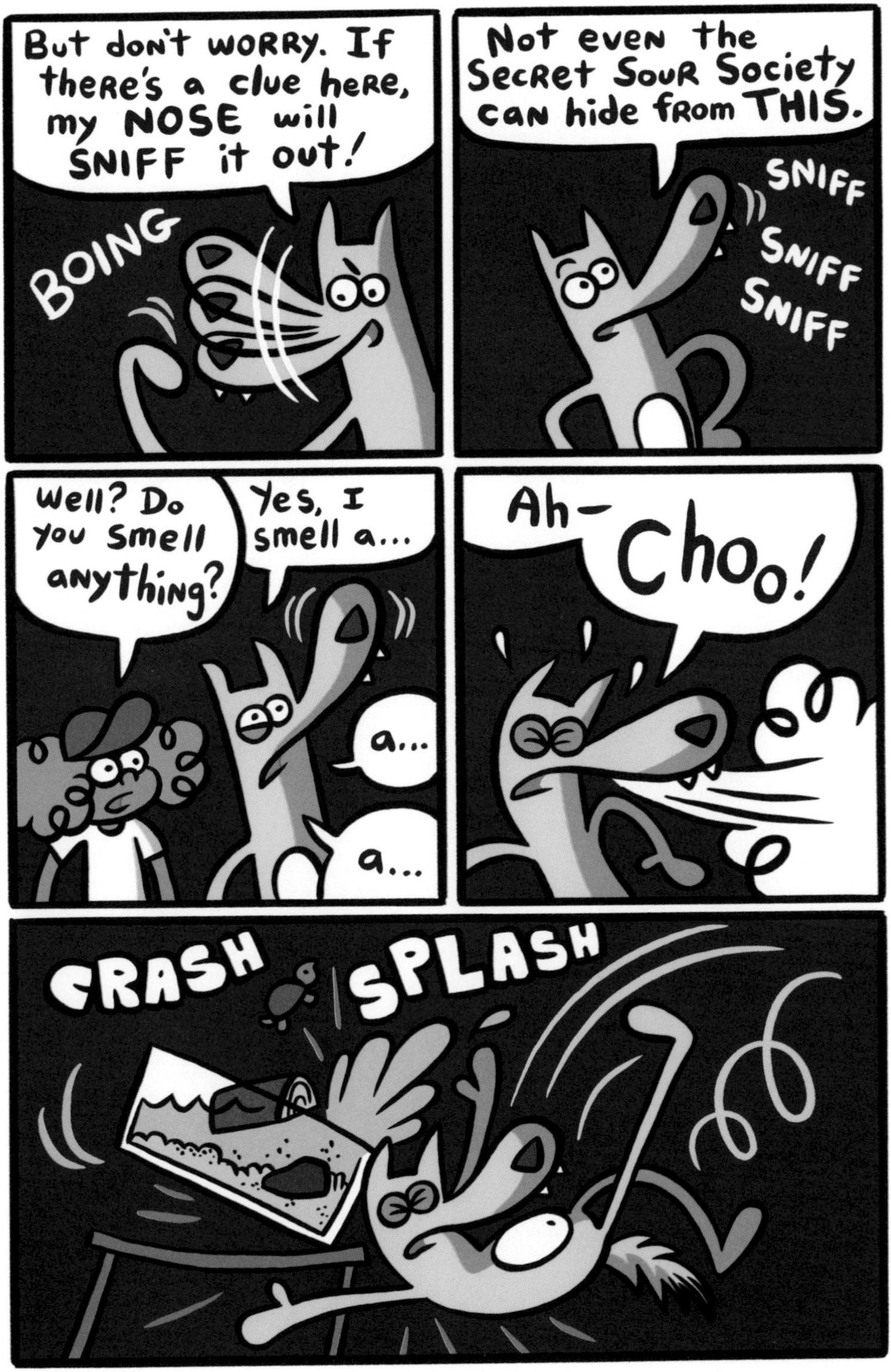

But don't WORRY. If there's a clue here, my NOSE will SNIFF it out!
BOING
Not even the Secret Sour Society can hide from THIS.
SNIFF
SNIFF
SNIFF
Well? Do you smell anything?
Yes, I smell a...
a...
a...
Ah-
Choo!
CRASH
SPLASH

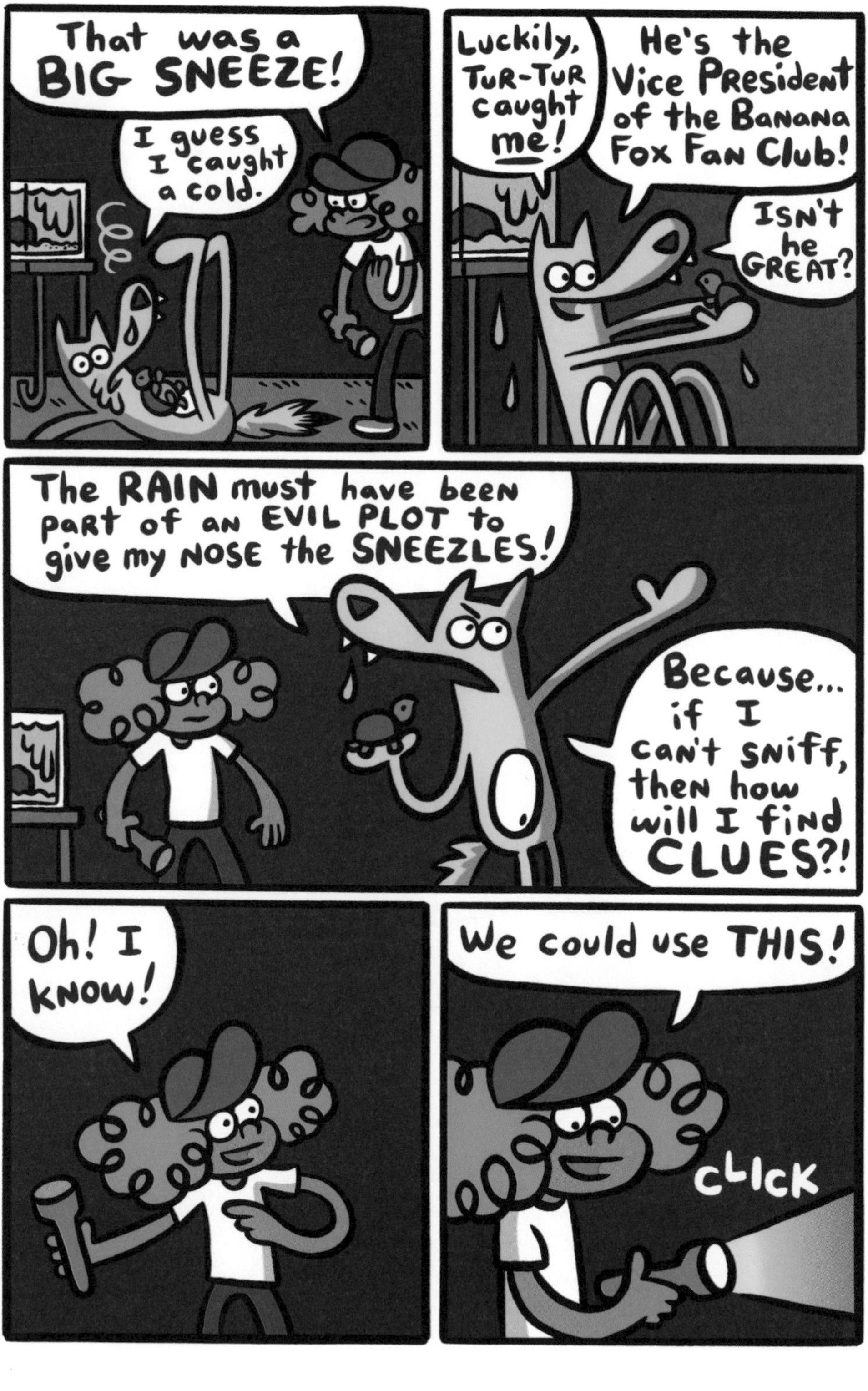

That was a BIG SNEEZE!
I guess I caught a cold.
Luckily, TUR-TUR caught me!
He's the Vice President of the Banana Fox Fan Club!
ISN'T he GREAT?
The RAIN must have been part of an EVIL PLOT to give my NOSE the SNEEZLES!
Because... if I can't sniff, then how will I find CLUES?!
Oh! I KNOW!
We could use THIS!
CLICK

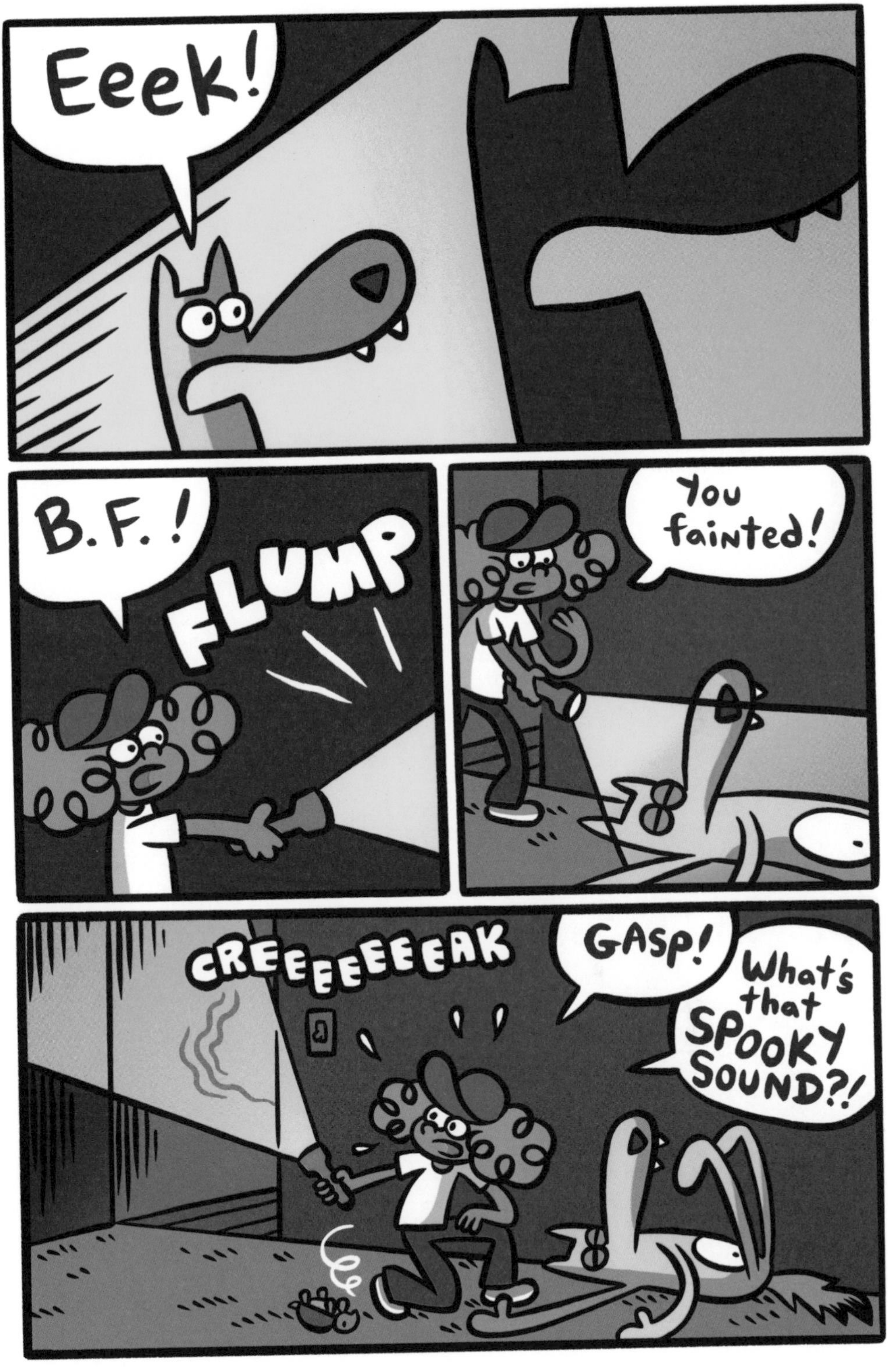
Eeek!
B.F.!
FLUMP
You fainted!
CREEEEEEEEAK
GASP!
What's that SPOOKY SOUND?!

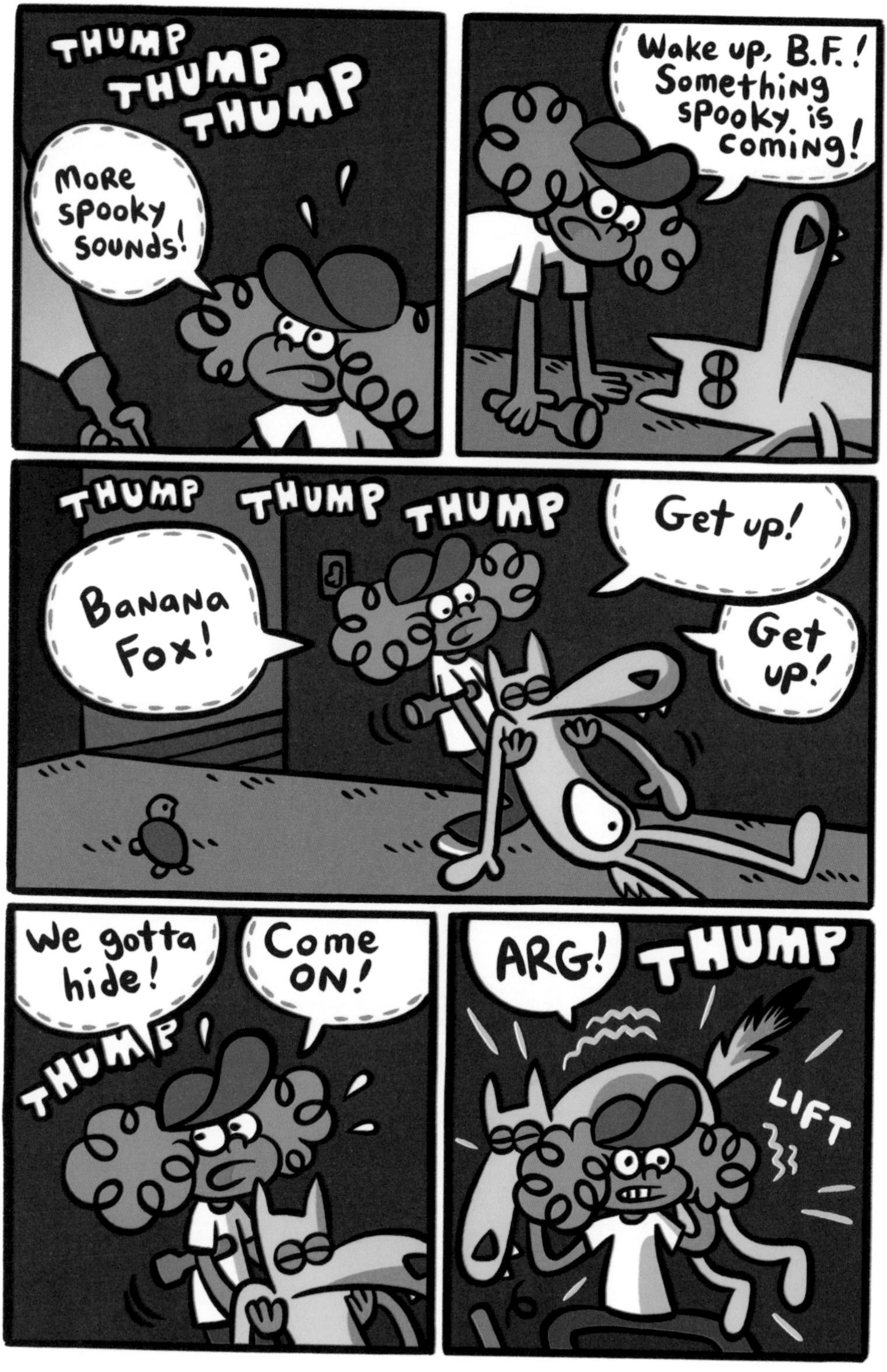
THUMP
THUMP
THUMP
More spooky sounds!
Wake up, B.F.! Something spooky is coming!
THUMP THUMP THUMP
Banana Fox!
Get up!
Get up!
We gotta hide!
Come ON!
THUMP
ARG!
THUMP
LIFT

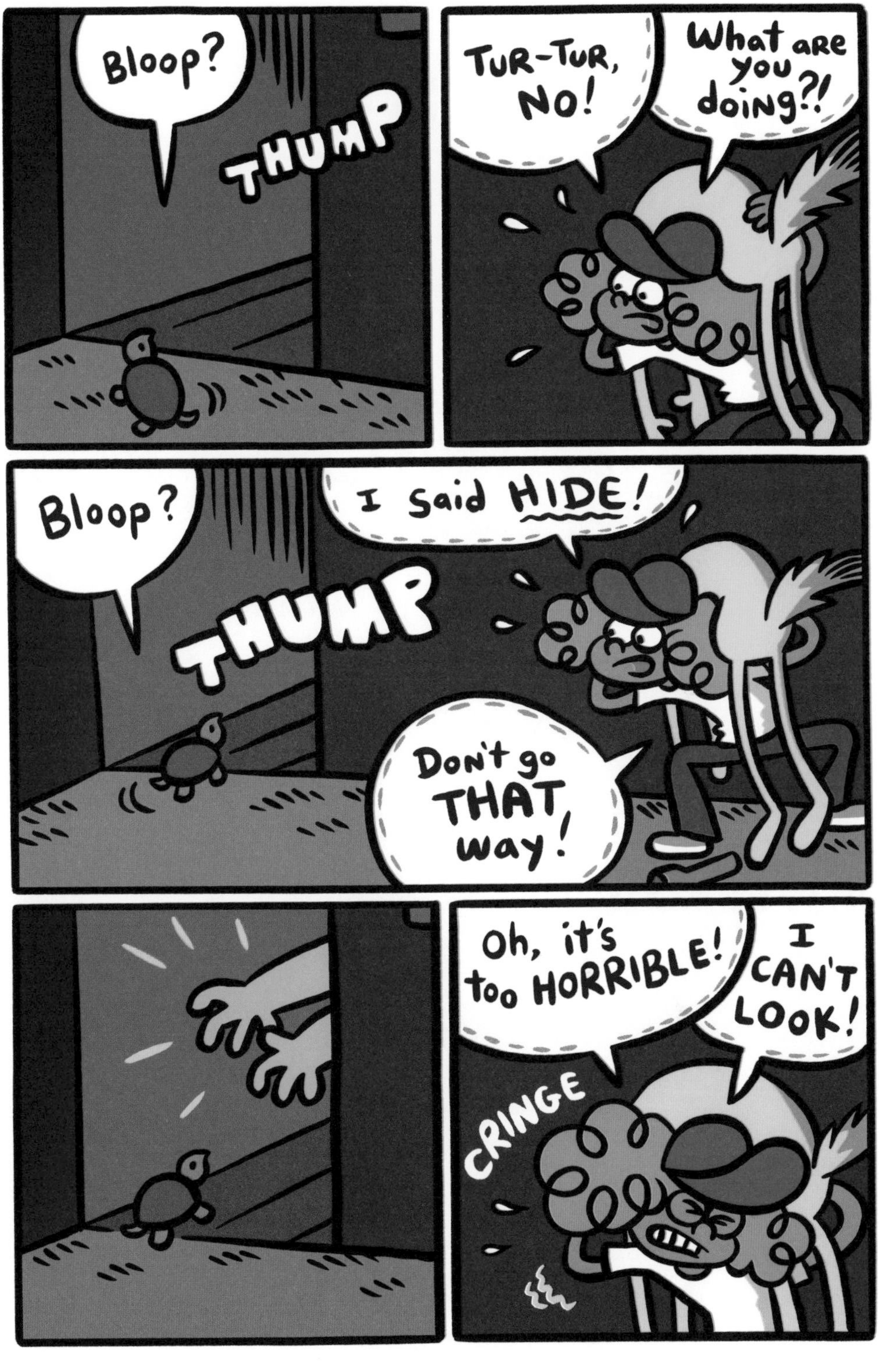
Bloop?
THUMP
TUR-TUR, NO!
What are you doing?!
Bloop?
I said HIDE!
THUMP
Don't go THAT way!
Oh, it's too HORRIBLE!
I CAN'T LOOK!
CRINGE

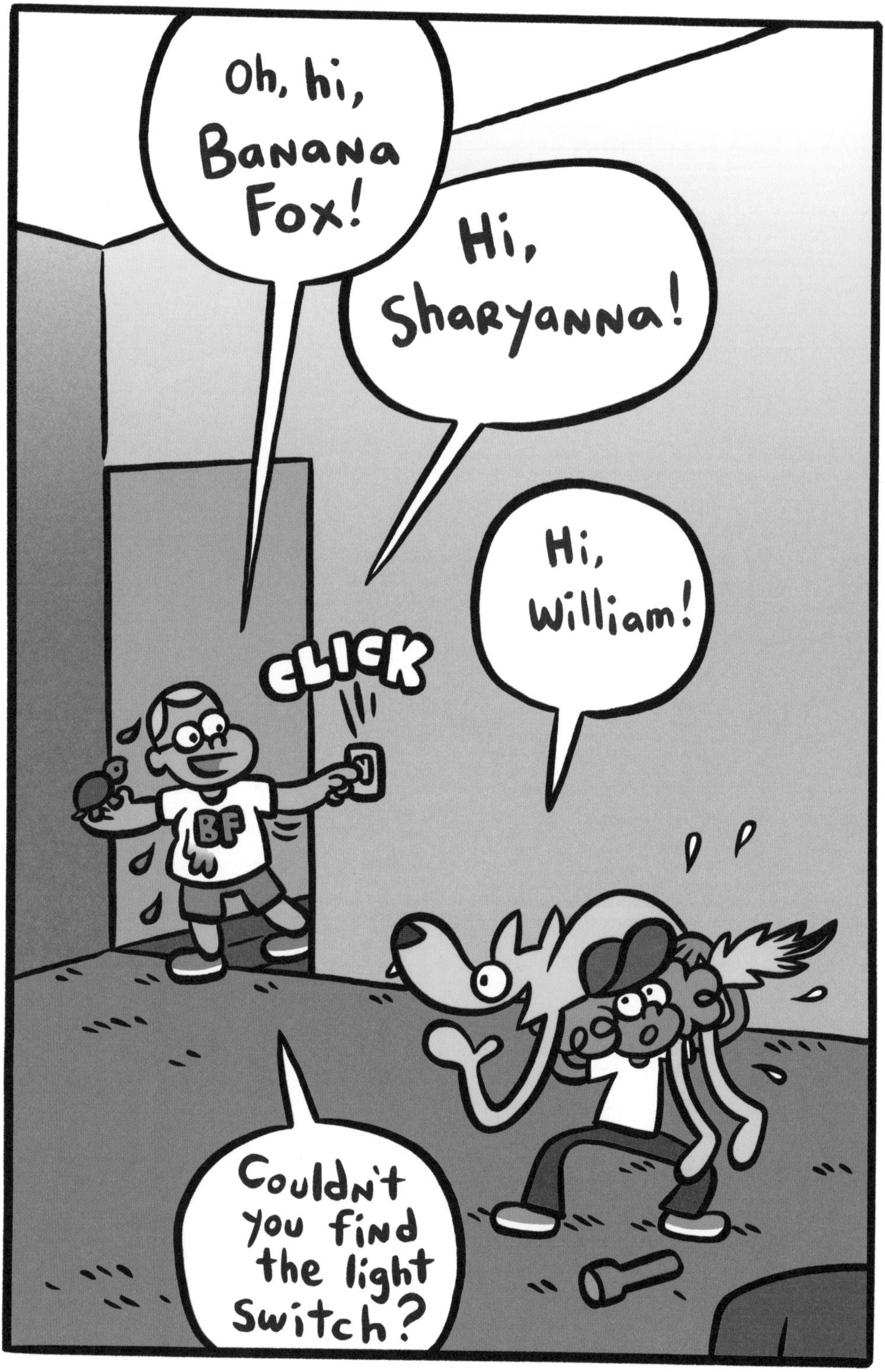
Oh, hi, Banana Fox!
Hi, Sharyanna!
CLICK
Hi, William!
Couldn't you find the light switch?

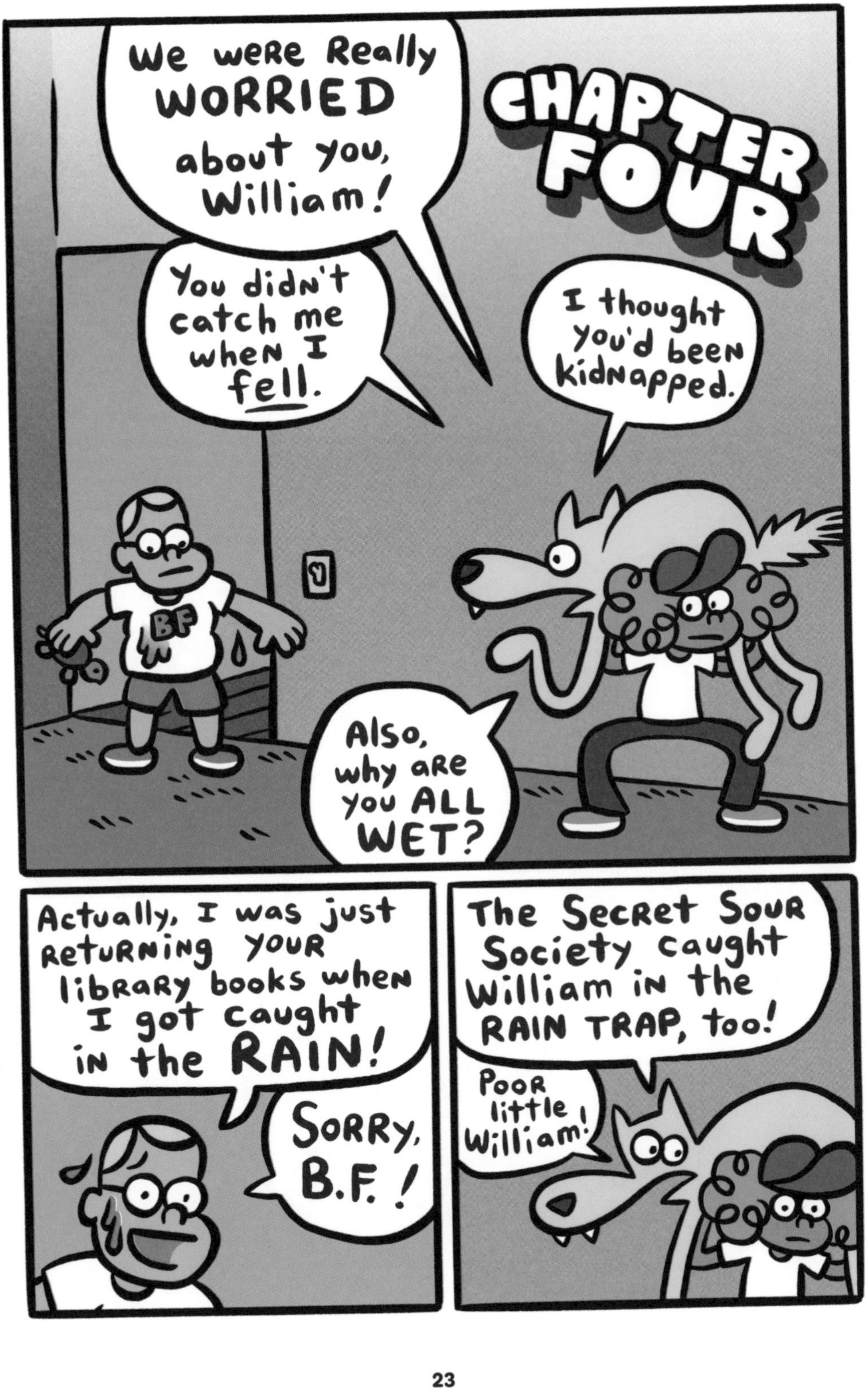

CHAPTER FOUR
We were Really WORRIED about you, William!
You didn't catch me when I fell.
I thought you'd been kidnapped.
Also, why are you ALL WET?
Actually, I was just returning YOUR library books when I got caught in the RAIN!
SORRY, B.F.!
The Secret Sour Society caught William in the RAIN TRAP, too!
Poor little William!

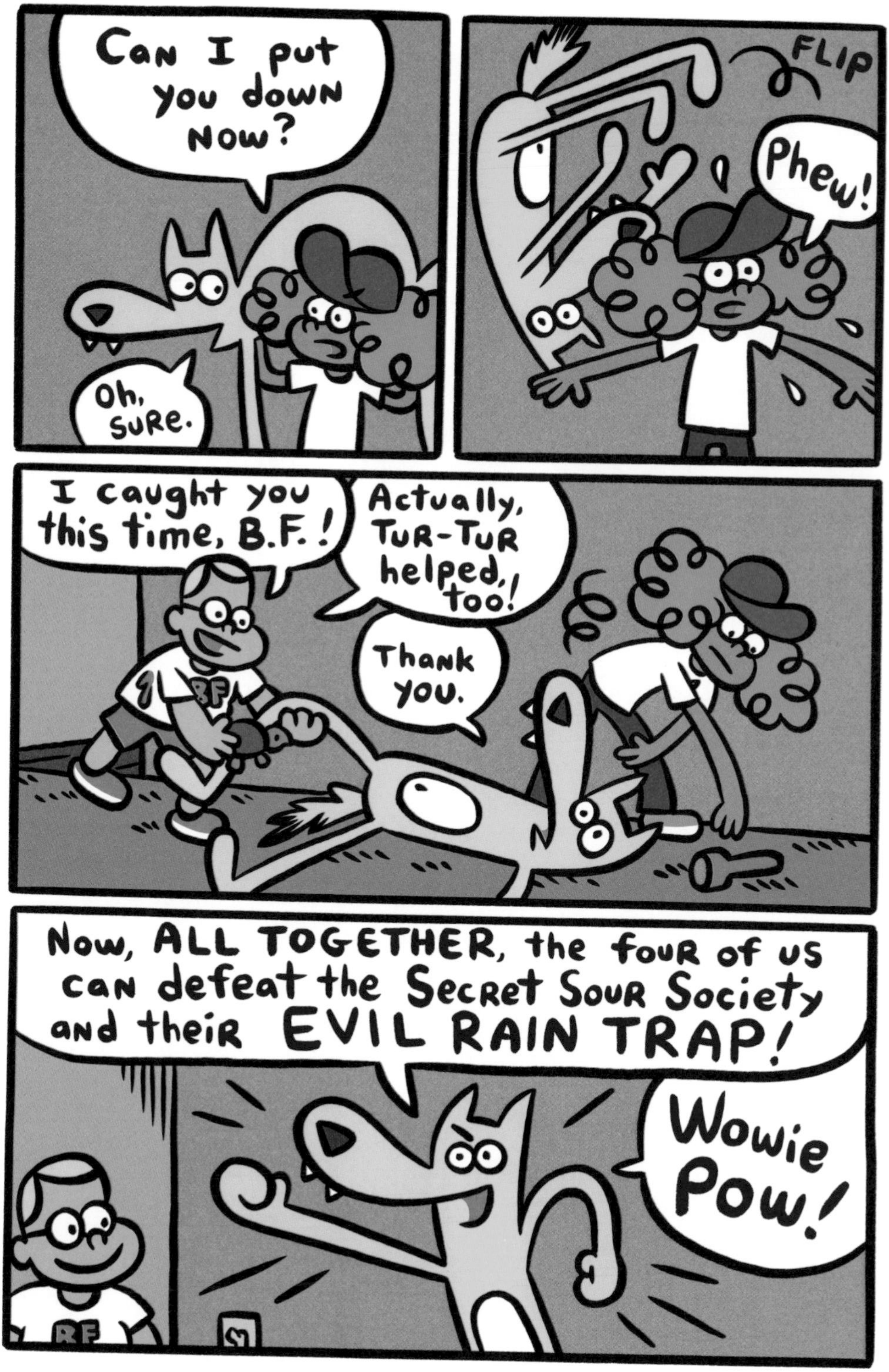
Can I put you down Now?
Oh, sure.
FLIP
Phew!
I caught you this time, B.F.!
Actually, Tur-Tur helped, too!
Thank you.
Now, ALL TOGETHER, the four of us can defeat the Secret Sour Society and their EVIL RAIN TRAP!
Wowie Pow!
BF

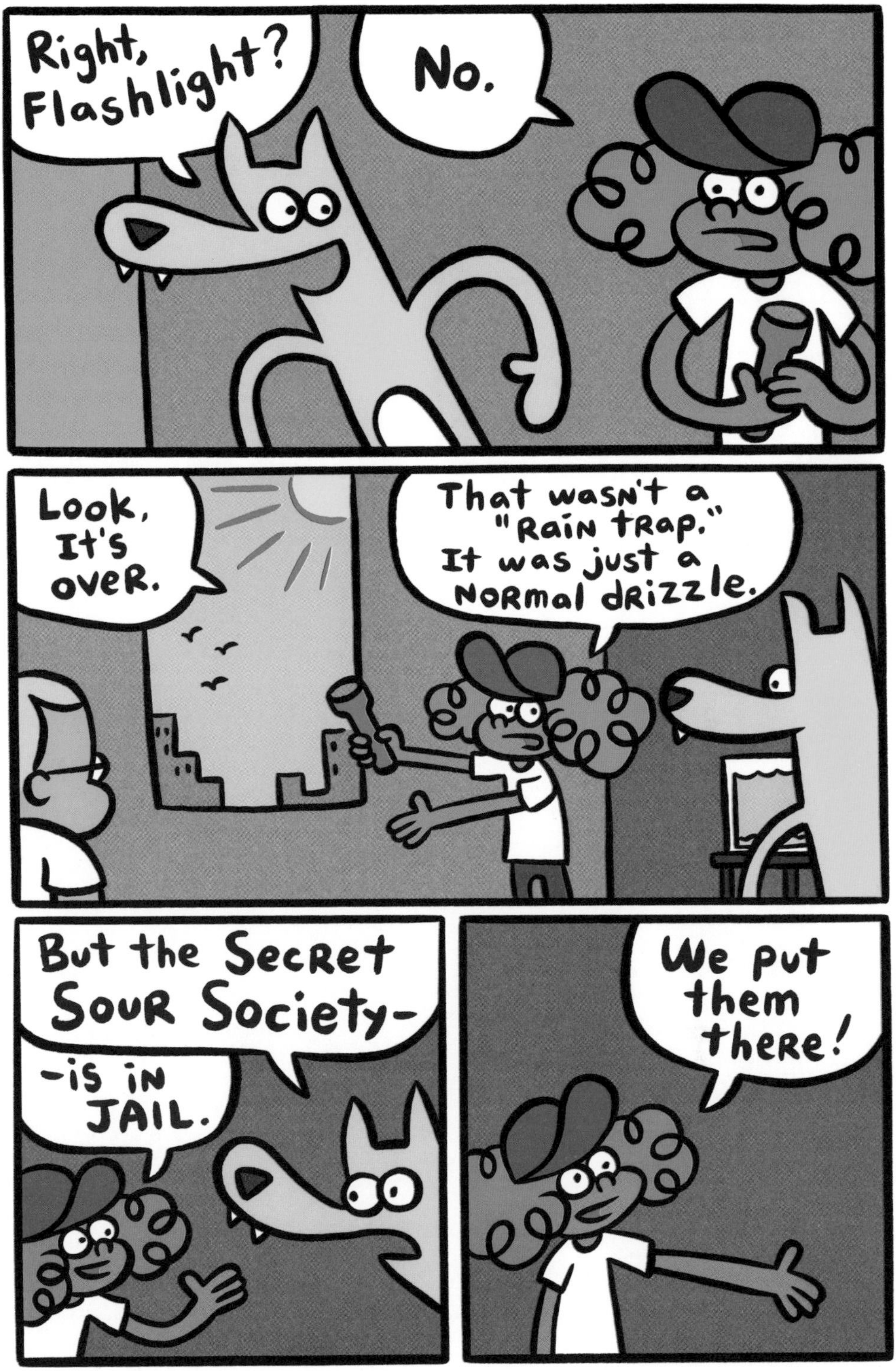
Right, Flashlight?
No.
Look, It's over.
That wasn't a "Rain trap." It was just a normal drizzle.
But the Secret Sour Society-
-is in JAIL.
We put them there!

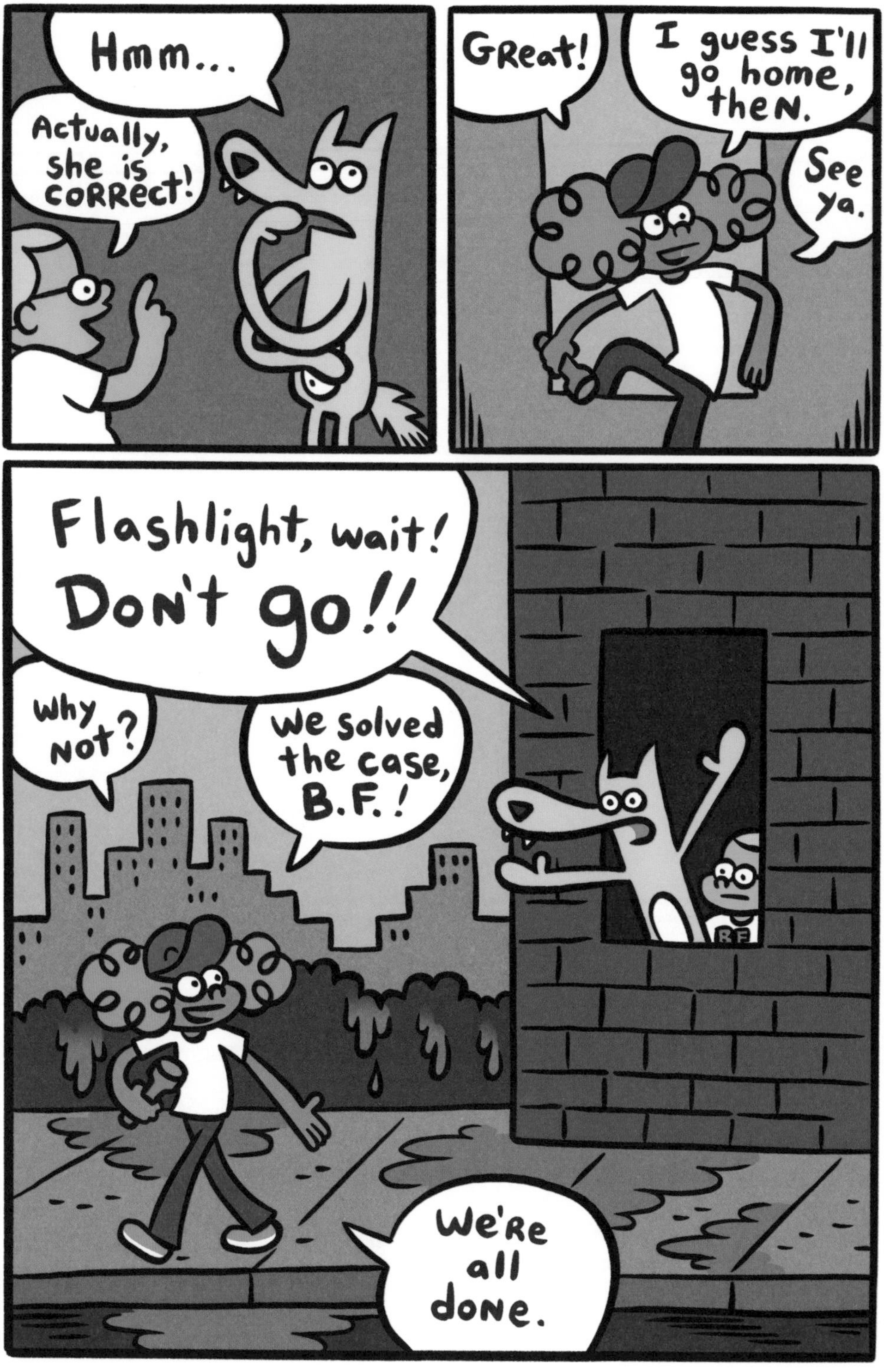
Hmm...
Actually, she is correct!
Great!
I guess I'll go home, then.
See ya.
Flashlight, wait! Don't go!!
Why not?
We solved the case, B.F.!
We're all done.

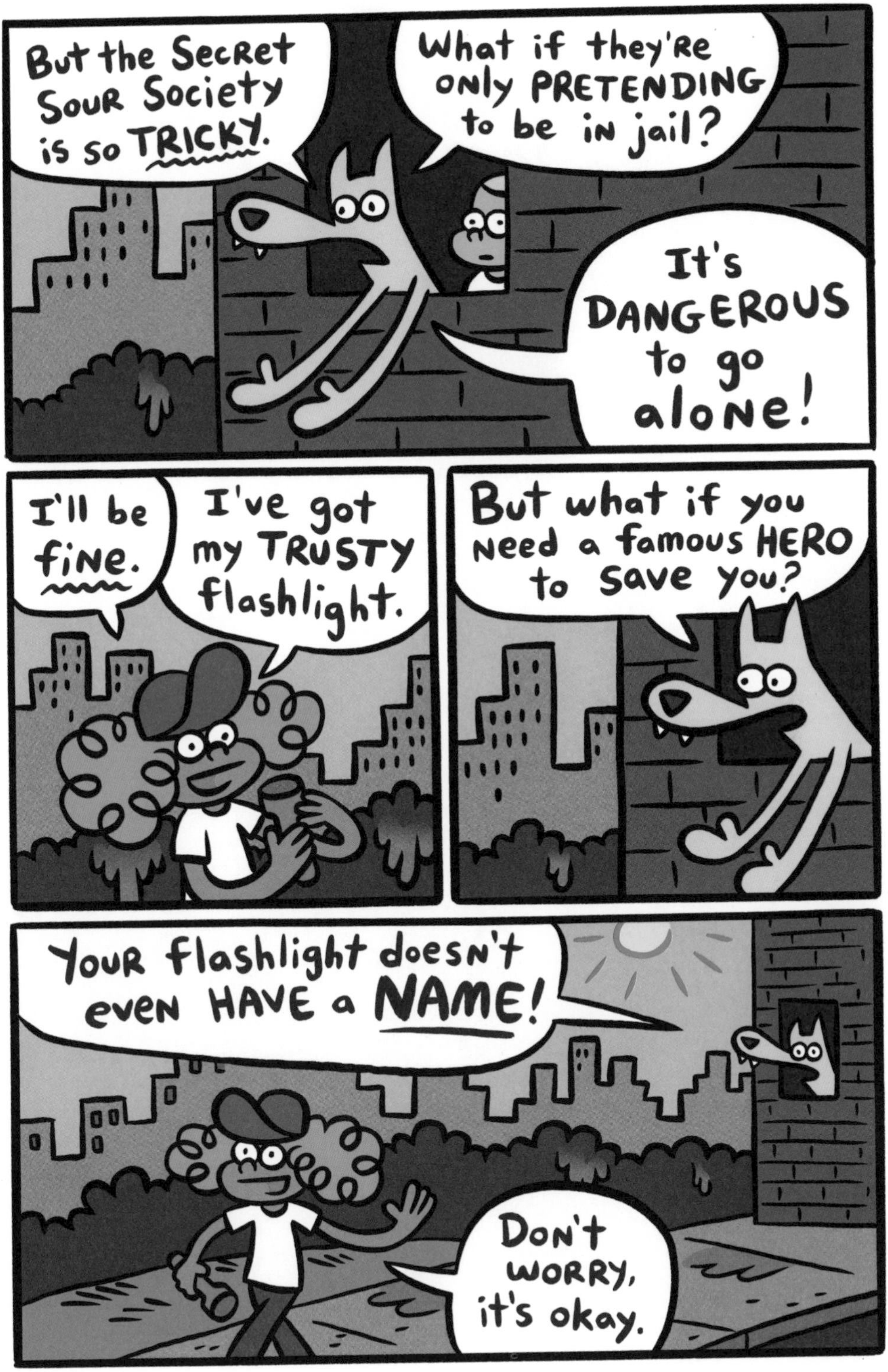
But the Secret Sour Society is so TRICKY.
What if they're only PRETENDING to be in jail?
It's DANGEROUS to go alone!
I'll be fine.
I've got my TRUSTY flashlight.
But what if you need a famous HERO to save you?
Your flashlight doesn't even HAVE a NAME!
Don't WORRY, it's okay.

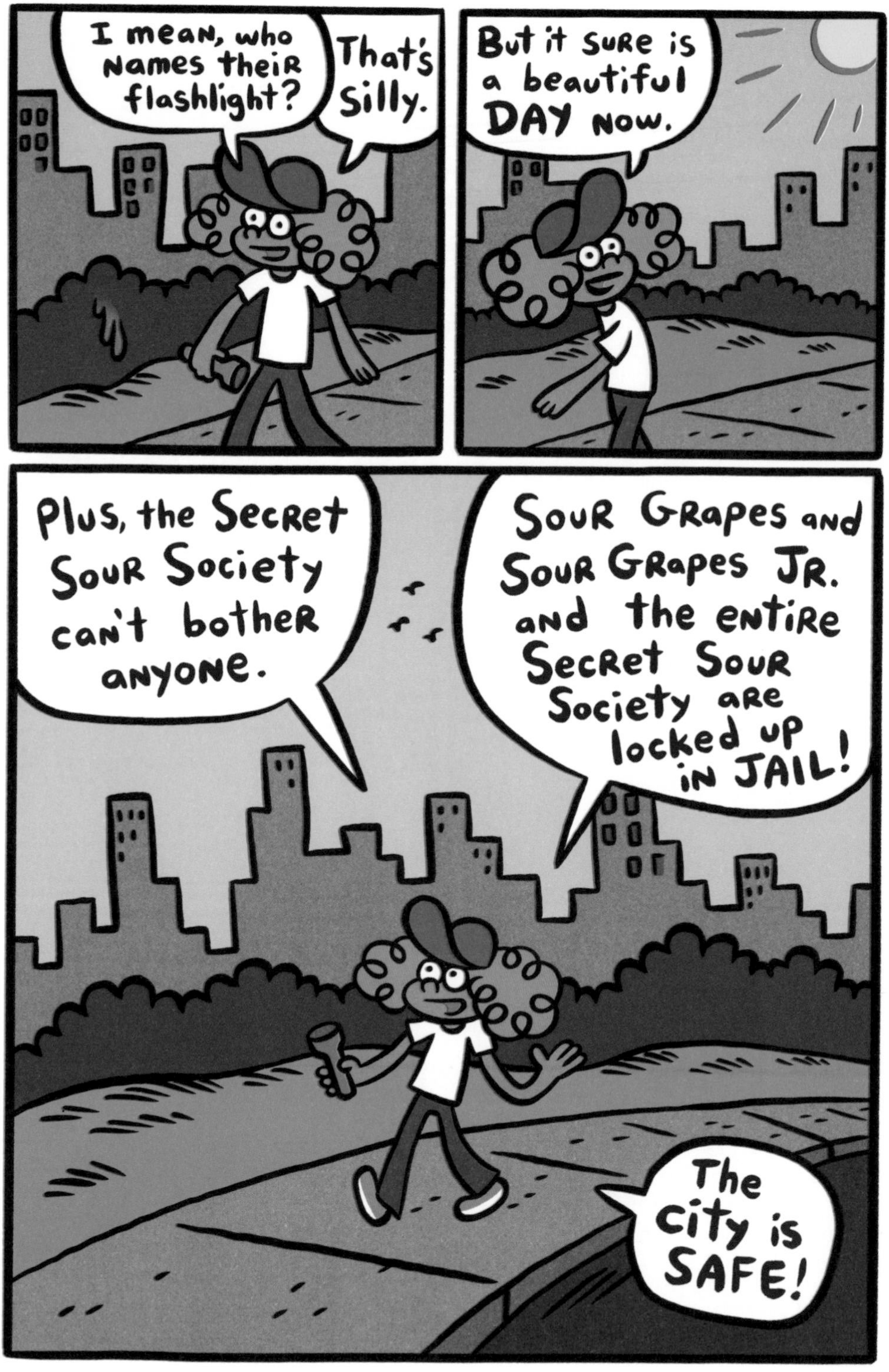
I mean, who names their flashlight?
That's silly.
But it sure is a beautiful DAY now.
Plus, the Secret Sour Society can't bother anyone.
Sour Grapes and Sour Grapes Jr. and the entire Secret Sour Society are locked up in JAIL!
The city is SAFE!

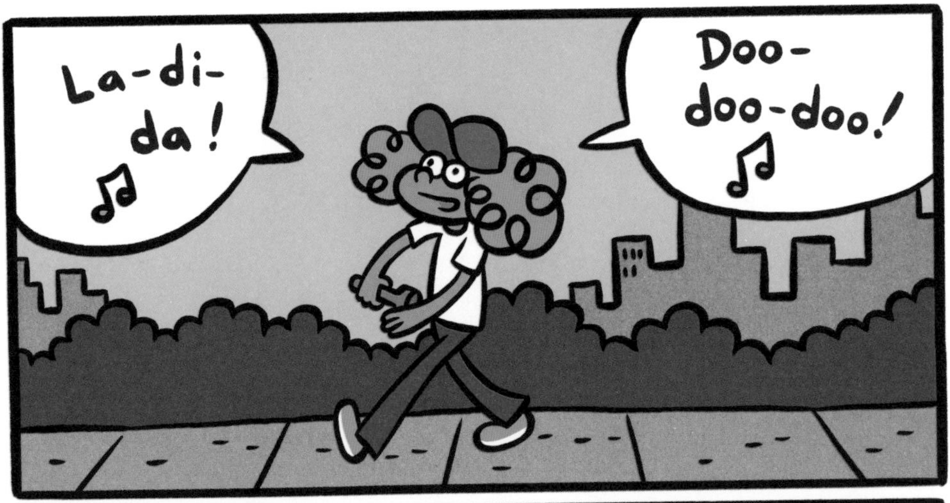
La-di-da!
Doo-doo-doo!

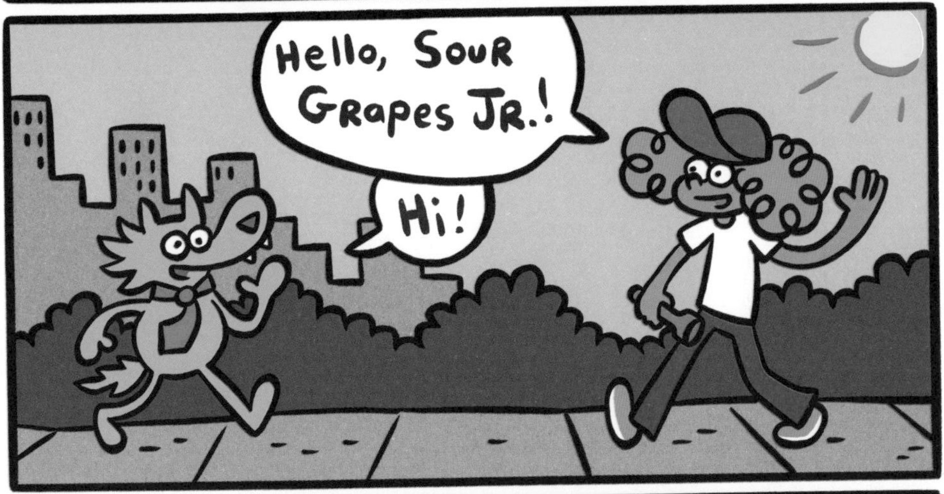
Hello, Sour Grapes Jr.!
Hi!

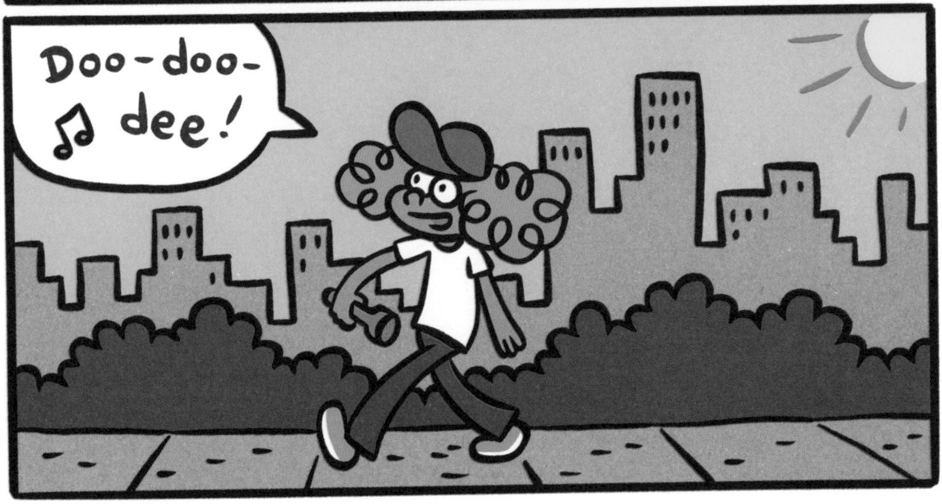
Doo-doo-dee!

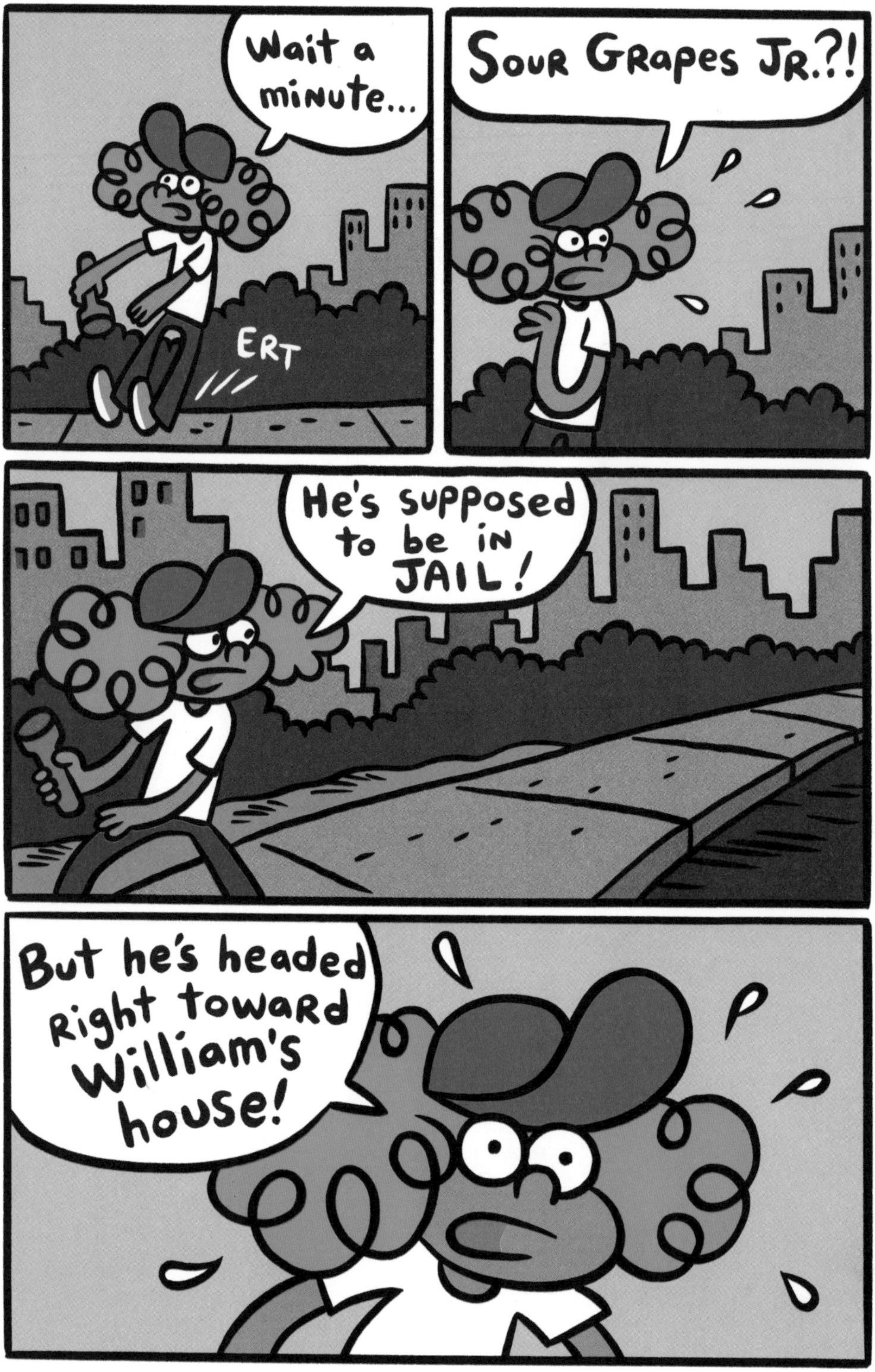
Wait a minute...
ERT
Sour Grapes Jr.?!
He's supposed to be in JAIL!
But he's headed right toward William's house!

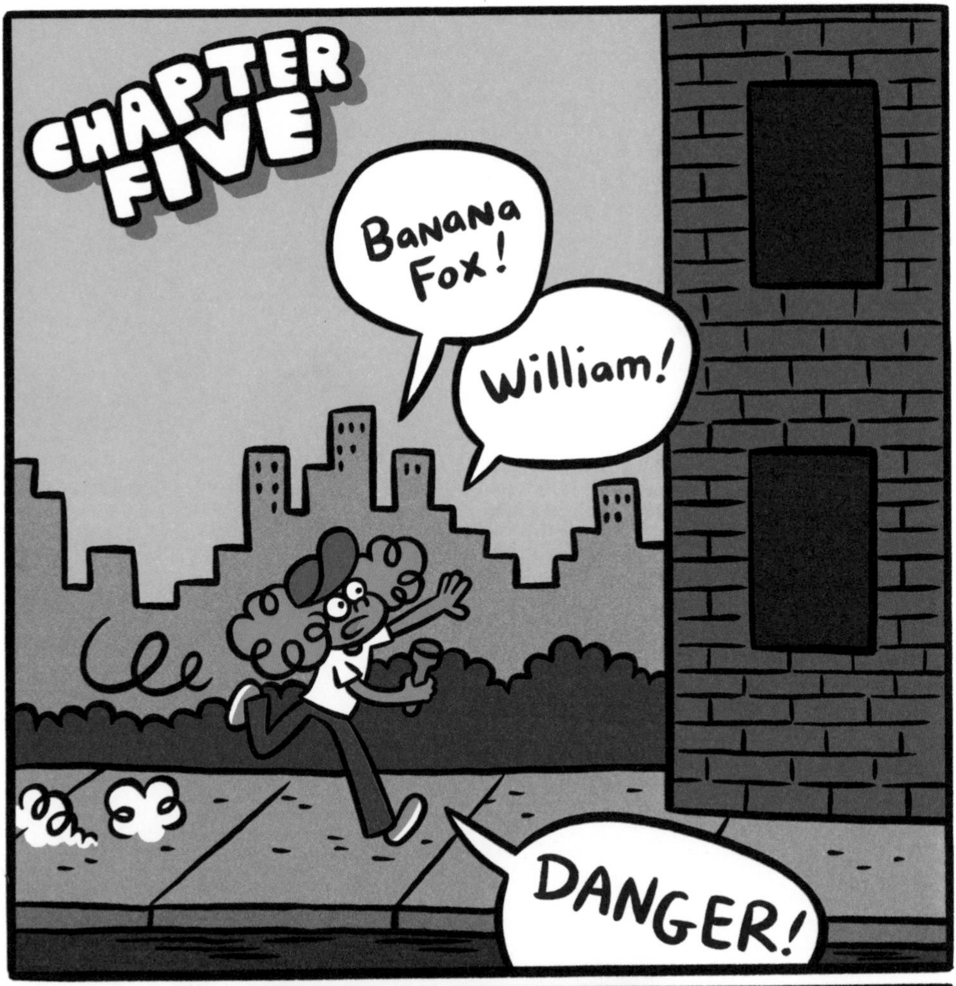
CHAPTER FIVE
Banana Fox!
William!
DANGER!

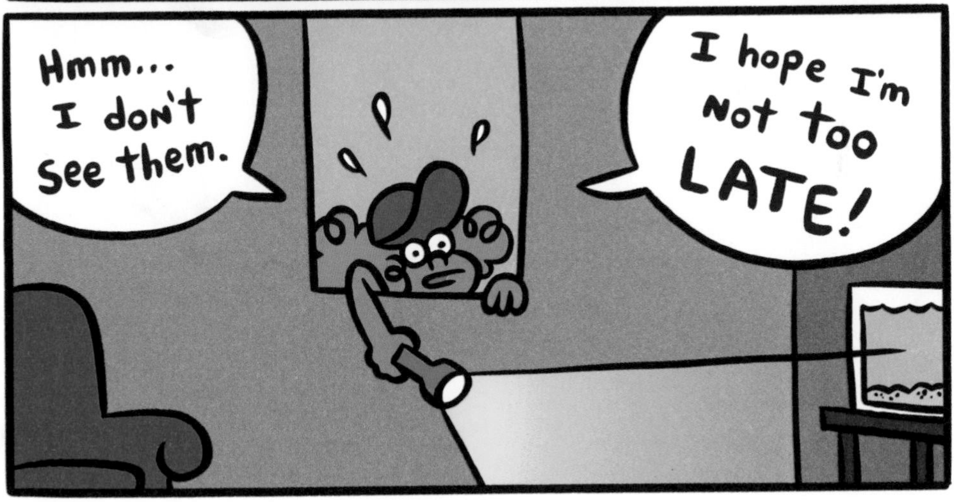
Hmm... I don't see them.
I hope I'm not too LATE!

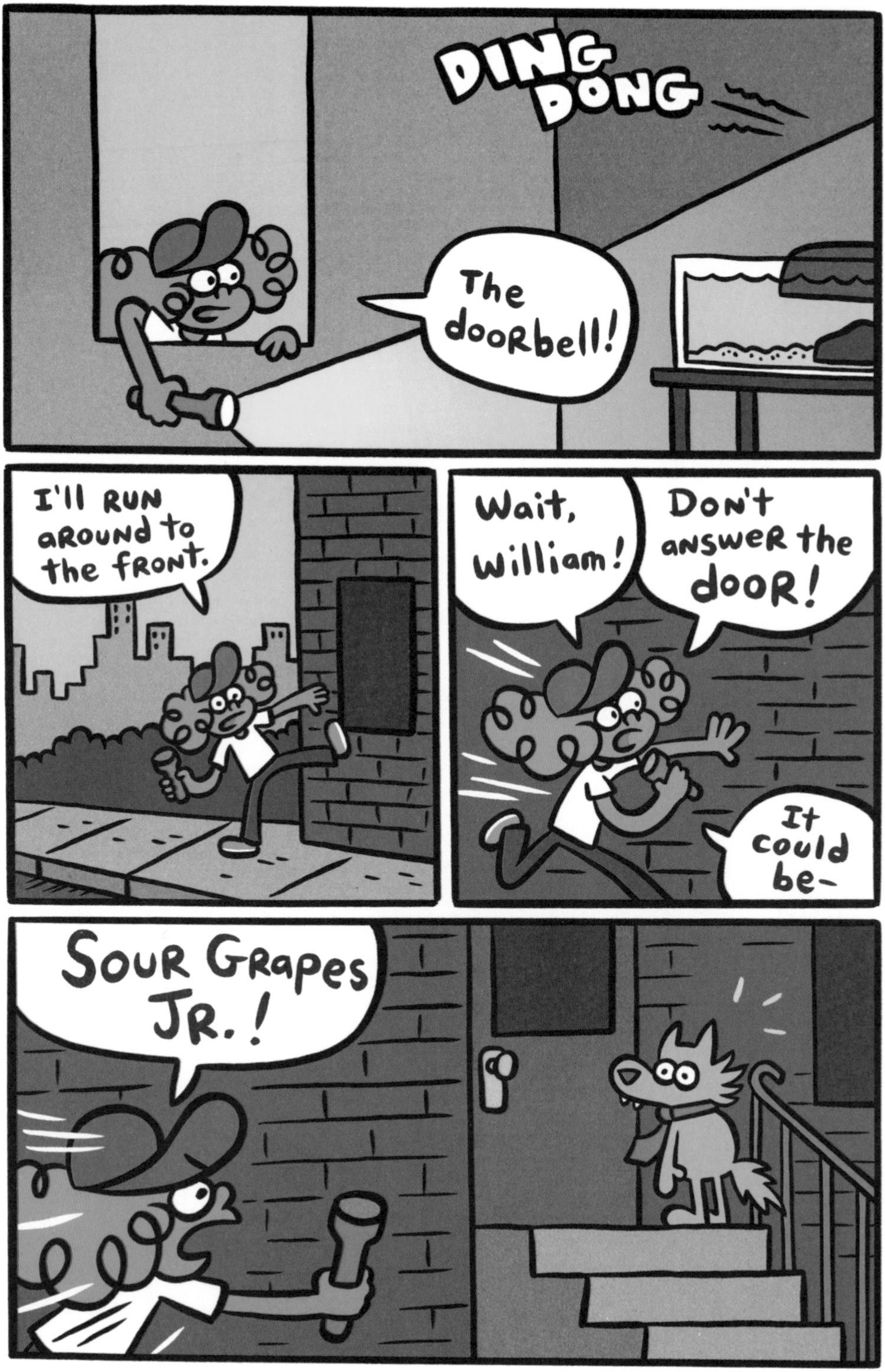
DING DONG
The doorbell!
I'll RUN around to the FRONT.
Wait, William!
Don't answer the door!
It could be-
Sour Grapes Jr.!

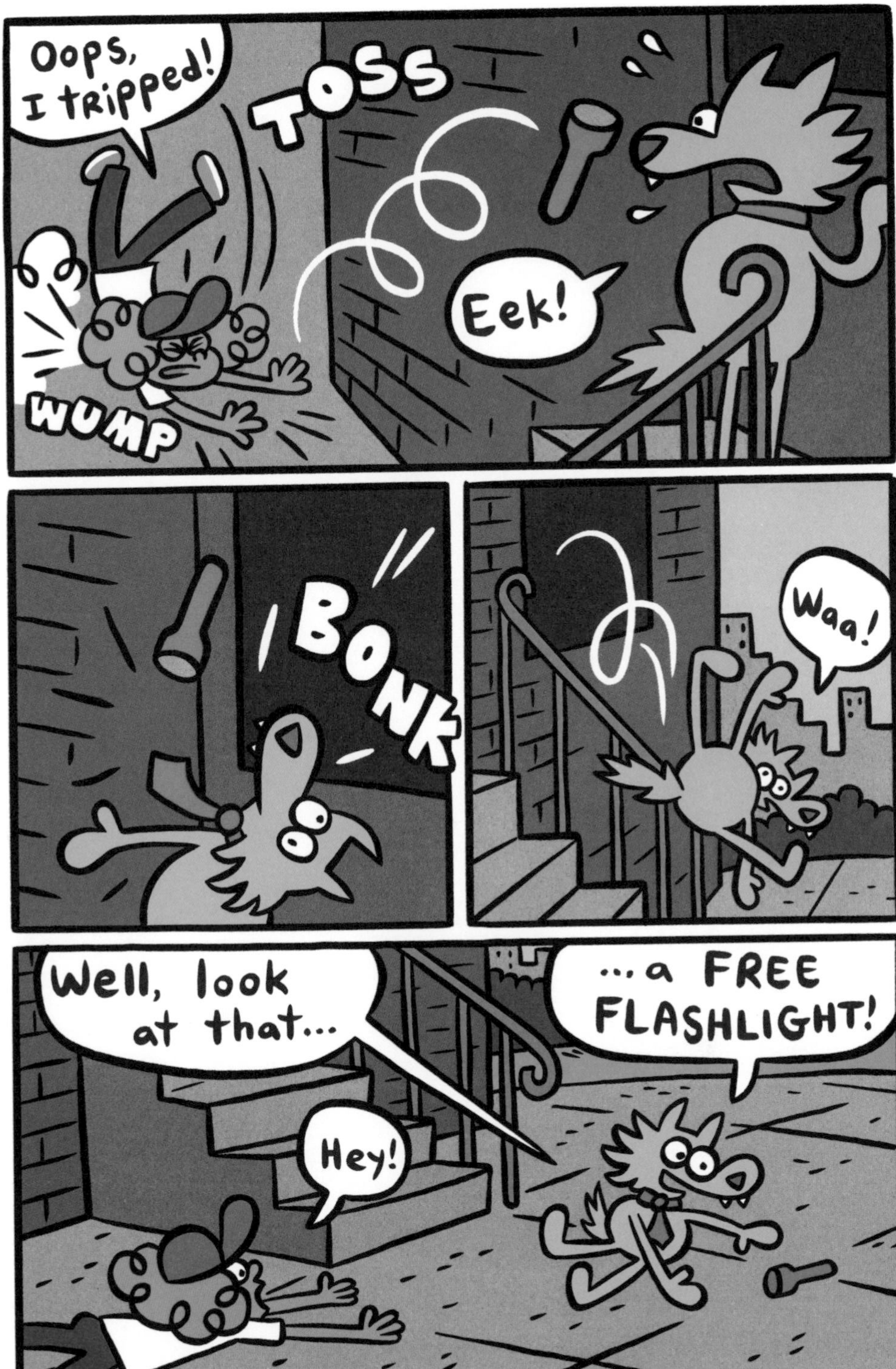
Oops, I tripped!
TOSS
Eek!
WUMP
BONK
Waa!
Well, look at that...
...a FREE FLASHLIGHT!
Hey!

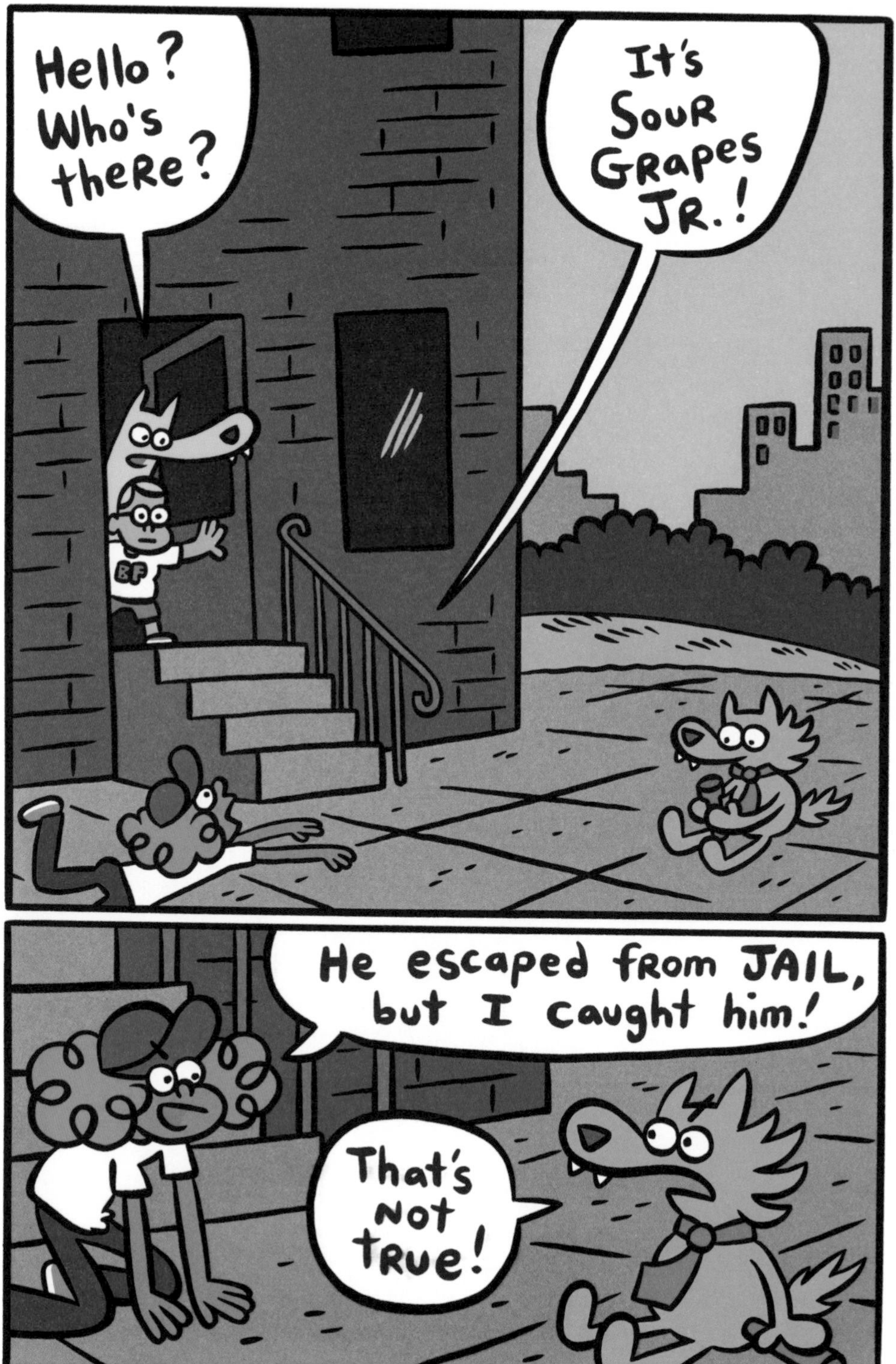
Hello? Who's there?
It's Sour Grapes Jr.!
He escaped from JAIL, but I caught him!
That's not true!

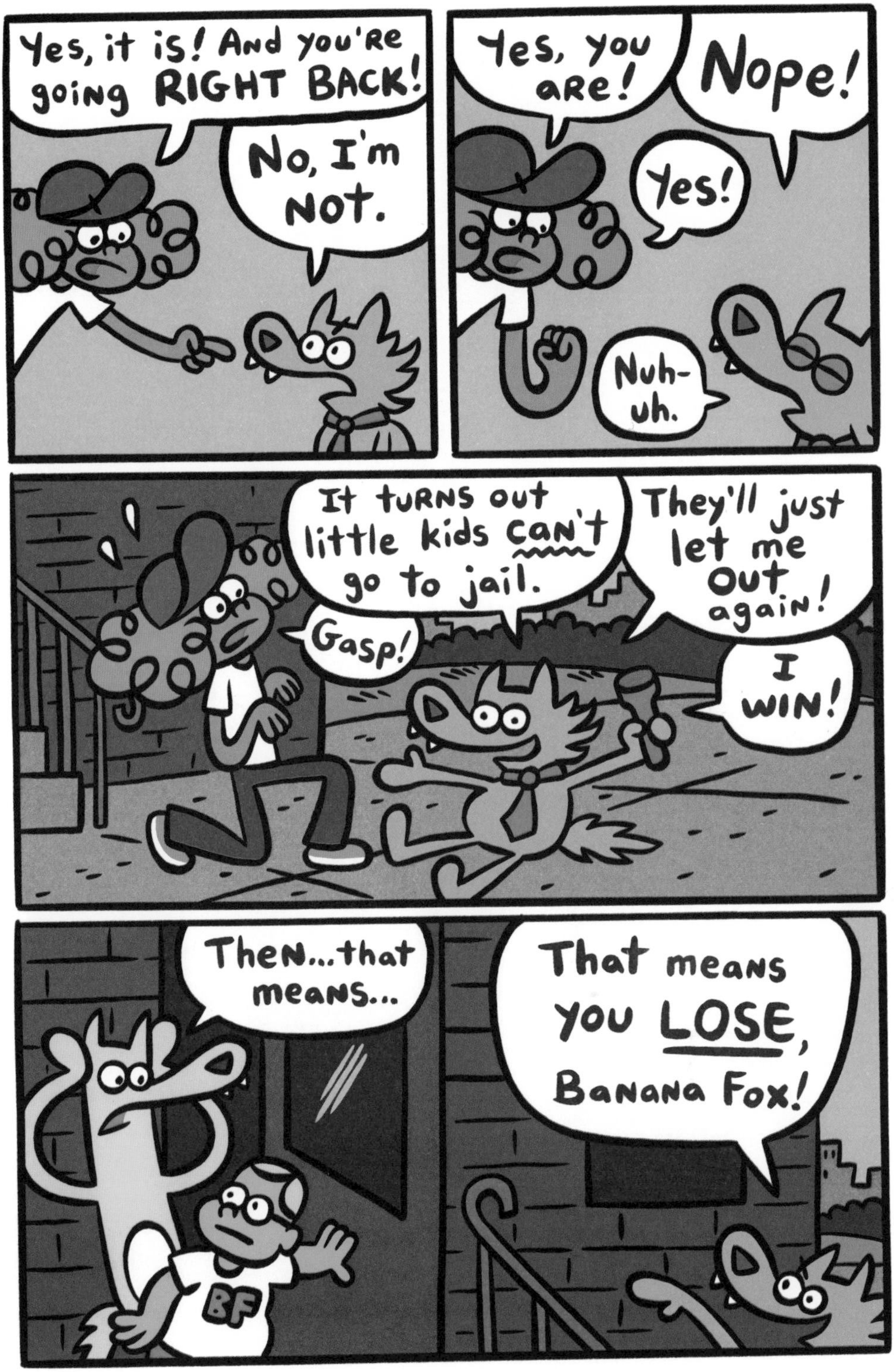
Yes, it is! And you're going RIGHT BACK!
No, I'm NOT.
Yes, you are!
Nope!
Yes!
Nuh-uh.
It turns out little kids can't go to jail.
Gasp!
They'll just let me out again!
I WIN!
Then...that means...
That means you LOSE, Banana Fox!

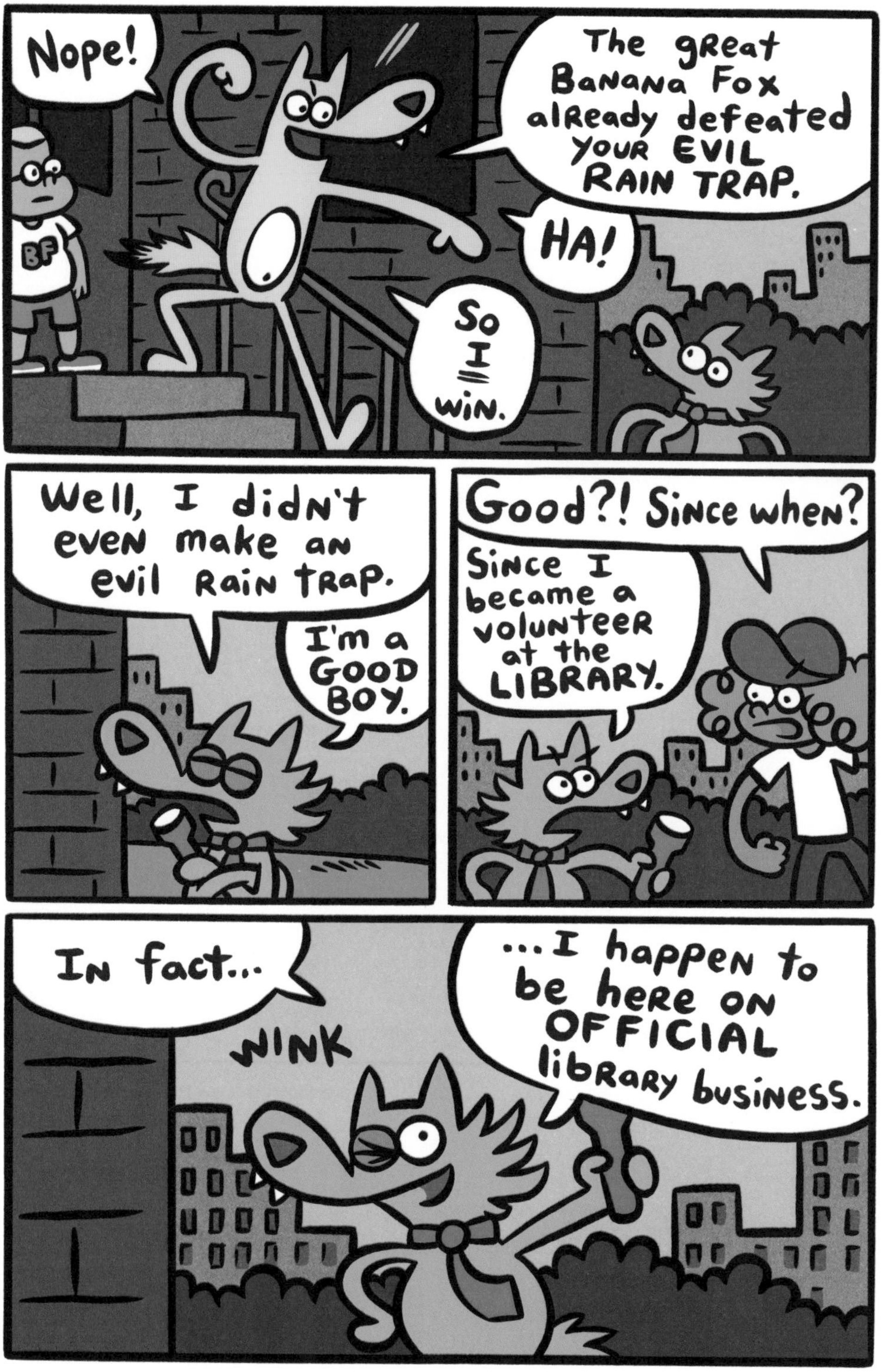
Nope!
The great Banana Fox already defeated your EVIL RAIN TRAP.
HA!
So I win.
Well, I didn't even make an evil rain trap.
I'm a GOOD BOY.
Good?! Since when?
Since I became a volunteer at the LIBRARY.
In fact...
WINK
...I happen to be here on OFFICIAL library business.

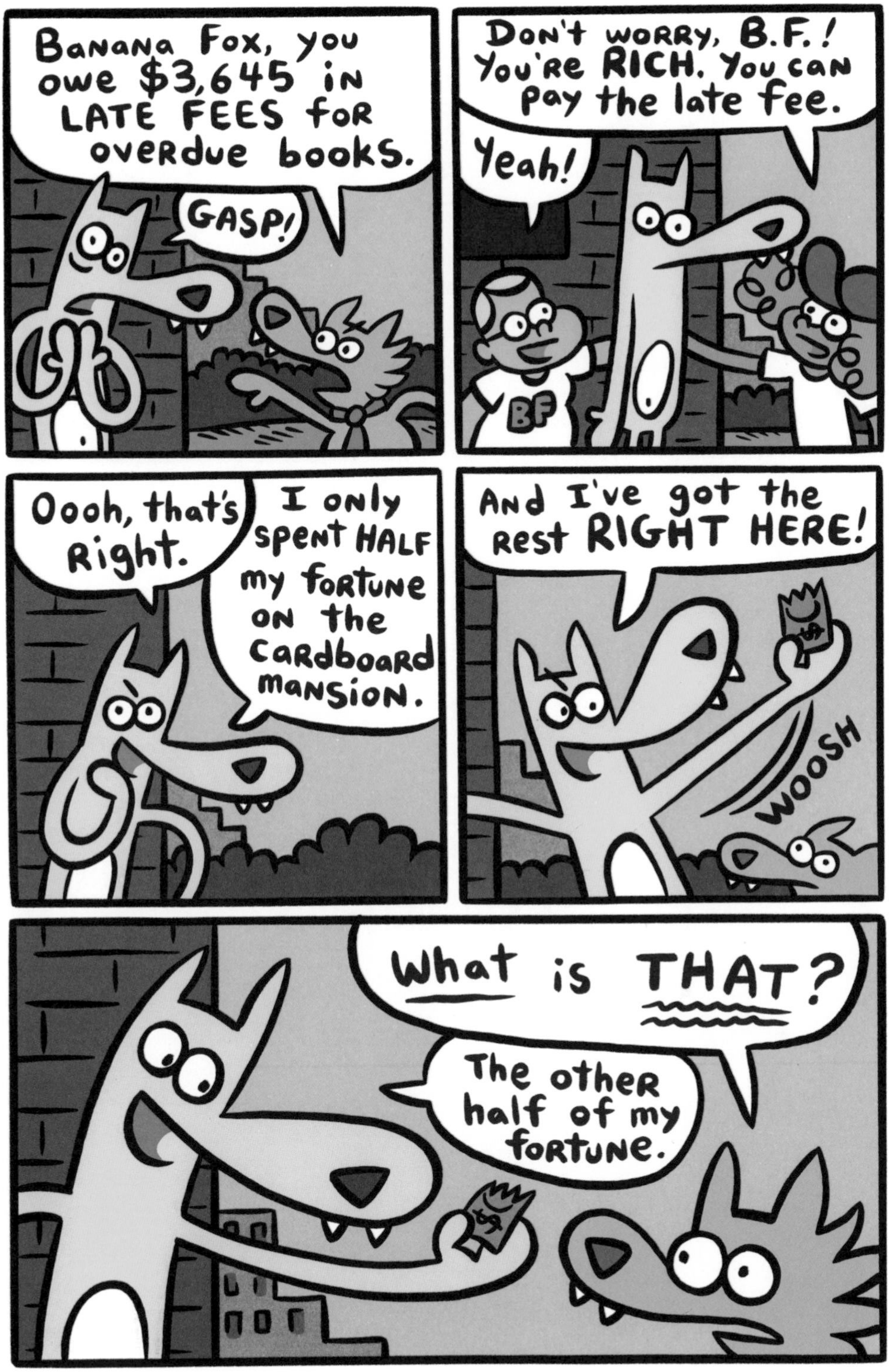
Banana Fox, you owe $3,645 in LATE FEES for overdue books.
GASP!
Don't worry, B.F.! You're RICH. You can pay the late fee.
Yeah!
BF
Oooh, that's Right.
I only spent HALF my fortune on the cardboard mansion.
And I've got the rest RIGHT HERE!
WOOSH
What is THAT?
The other half of my fortune.

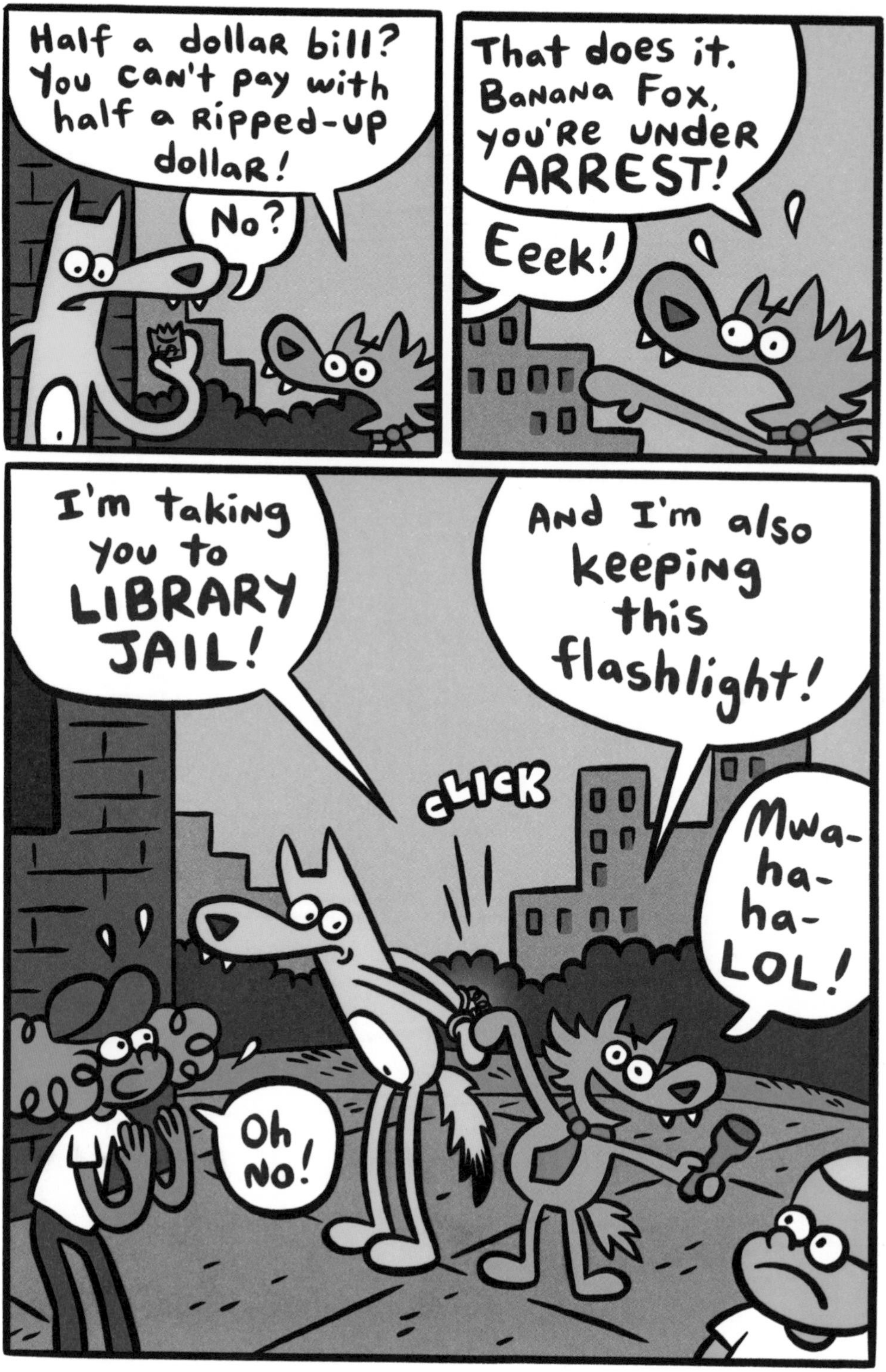
Half a dollar bill? You can't pay with half a ripped-up dollar!
No?
That does it. Banana Fox, you're under ARREST!
Eeek!
I'm taking you to LIBRARY JAIL!
And I'm also keeping this flashlight!
CLICK
Mwa-ha-ha-LOL!
Oh No!

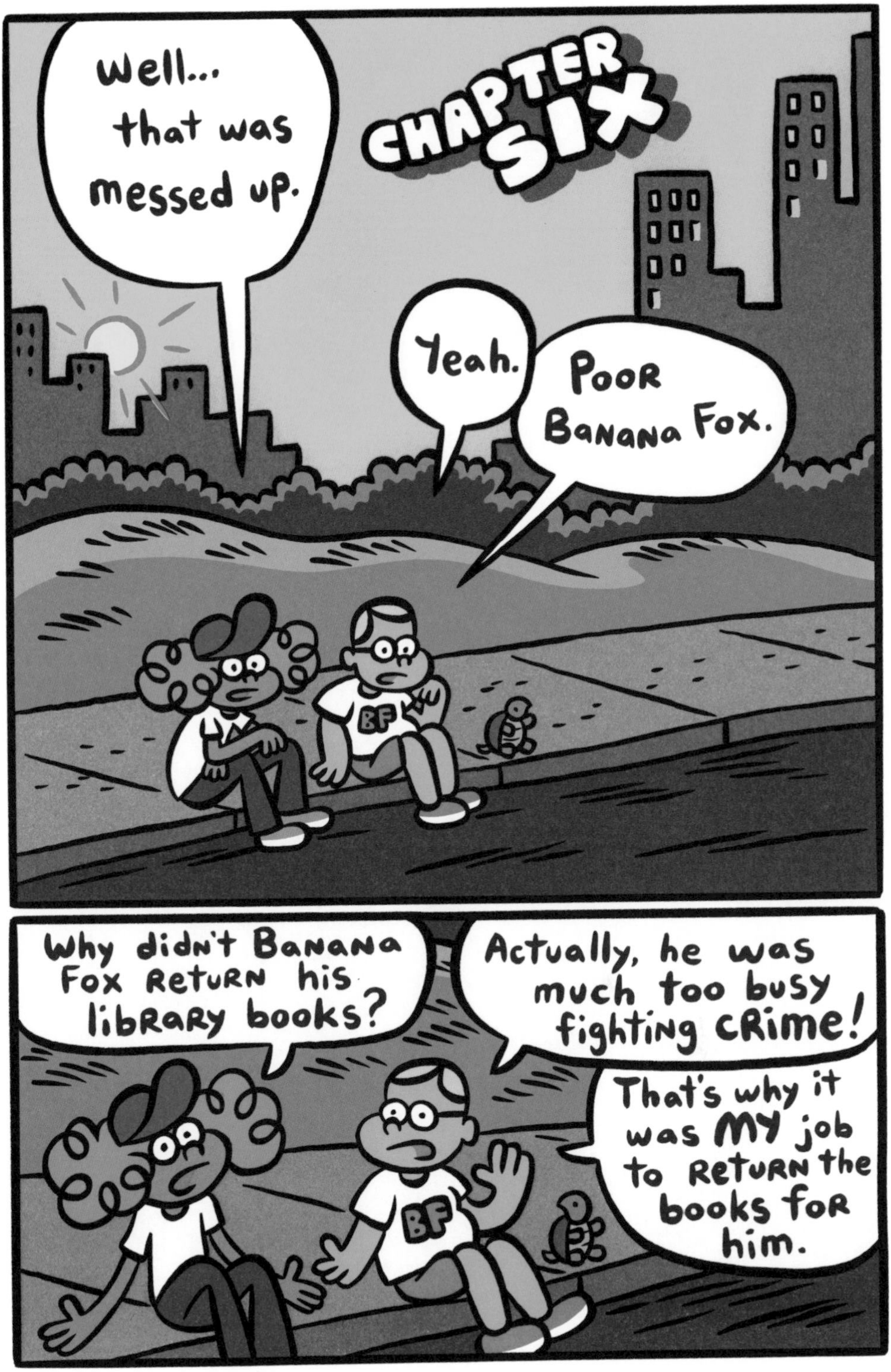
Well... that was messed up.
CHAPTER SIX
Yeah.
Poor Banana Fox.
Why didn't Banana Fox return his library books?
Actually, he was much too busy fighting crime!
That's why it was MY job to return the books for him.

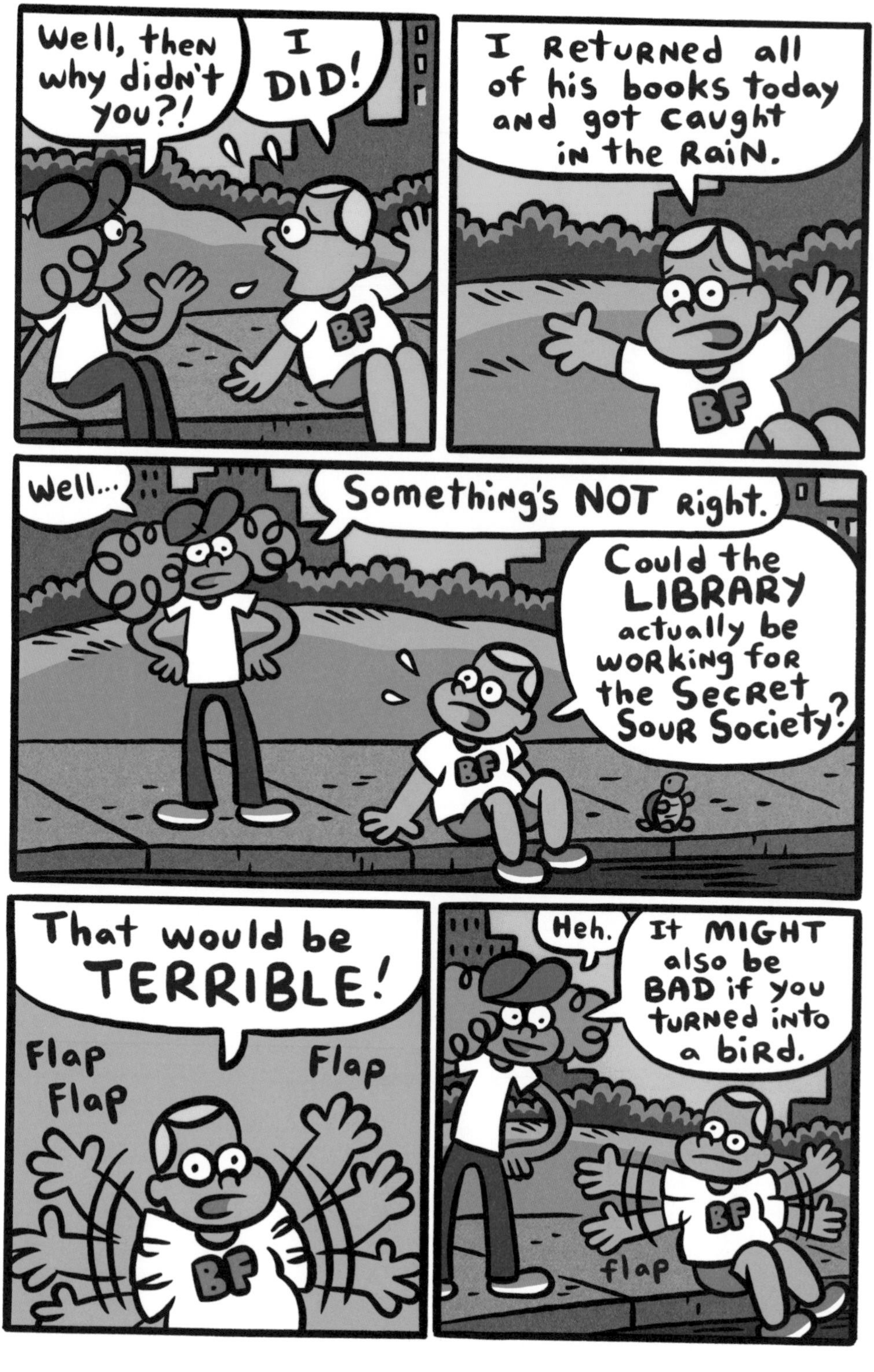
Well, then why didn't you?!
I DID!
I Returned all of his books today and got caught in the Rain.
Well...
Something's NOT Right.
Could the LIBRARY actually be working for the Secret Sour Society?
That would be TERRIBLE!
Flap
Flap
Flap
Heh.
It MIGHT also be BAD if you turned into a bird.
flap

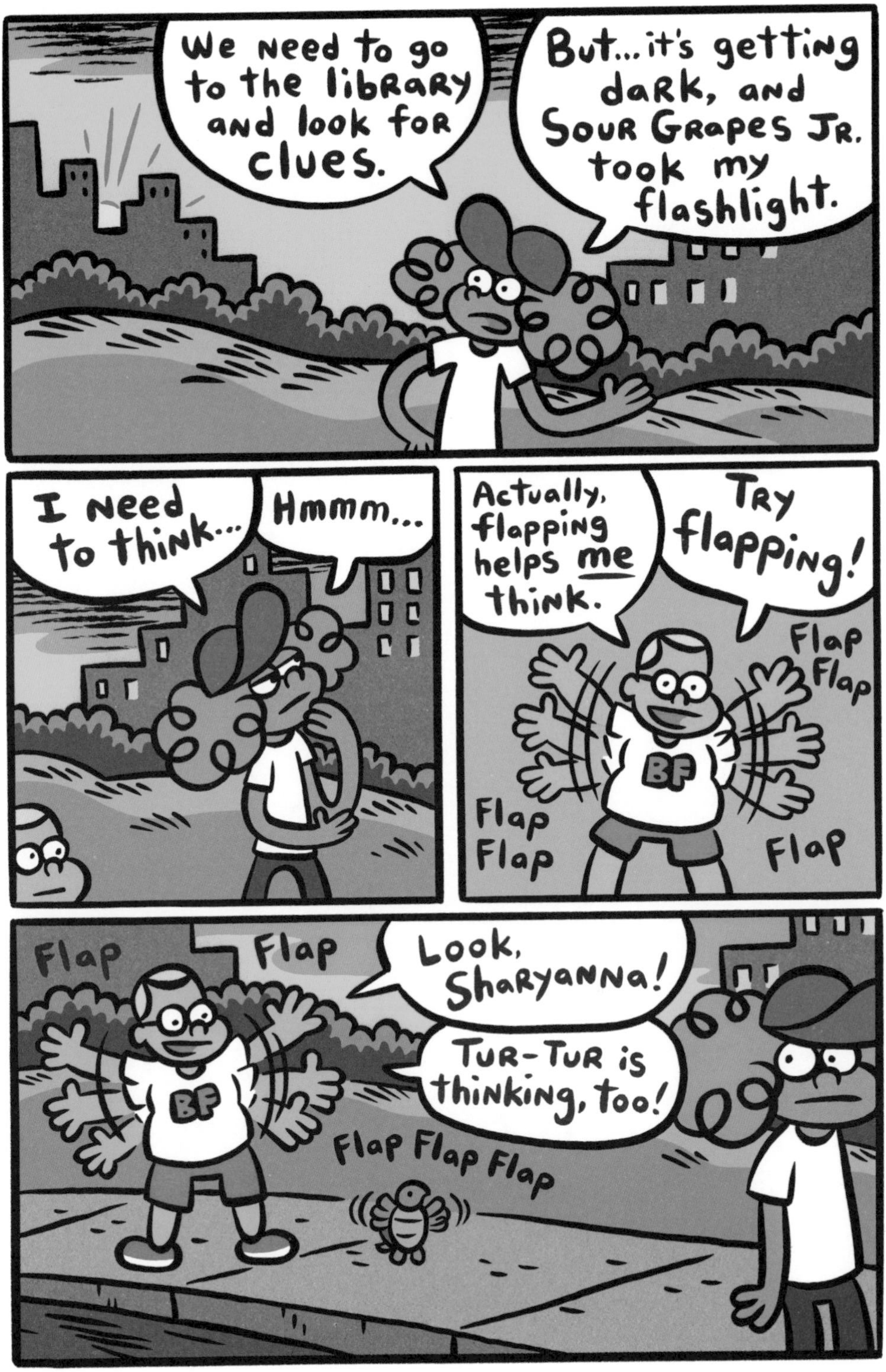
We need to go to the library and look for clues.
But... it's getting dark, and Sour Grapes Jr. took my flashlight.
I need to think...
Hmmm...
Actually, flapping helps me think.
Try flapping!
Flap
Flap
Flap
Flap
Flap
Flap
Flap
Look, Sharyanna!
Tur-Tur is thinking, too!
Flap Flap Flap

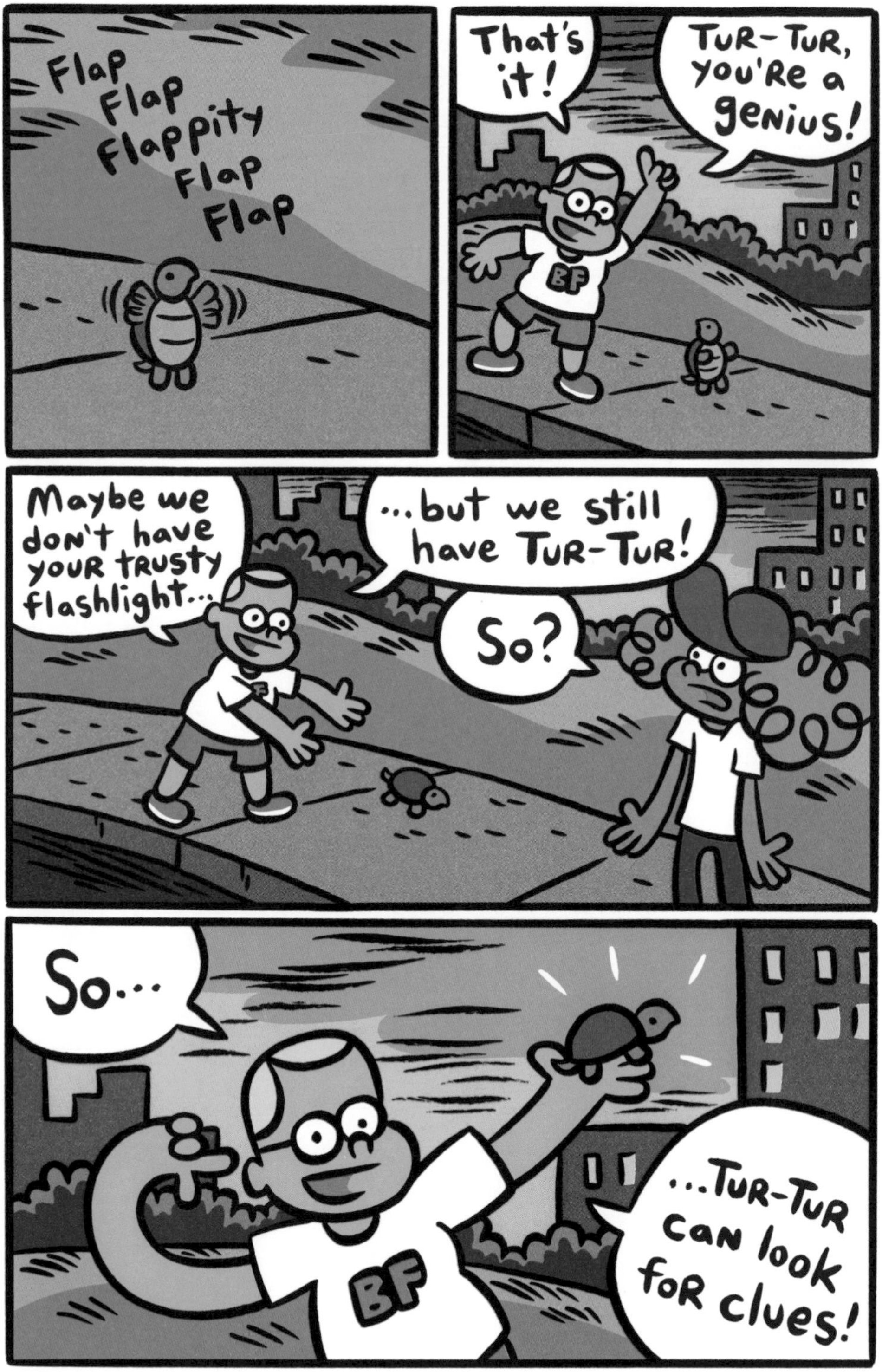
Flap
Flap
Flappity
Flap
Flap
That's it!
TUR-TUR, you're a genius!
Maybe we don't have your trusty flashlight...
...but we still have TUR-TUR!
So?
So...
...TUR-TUR can look for clues!

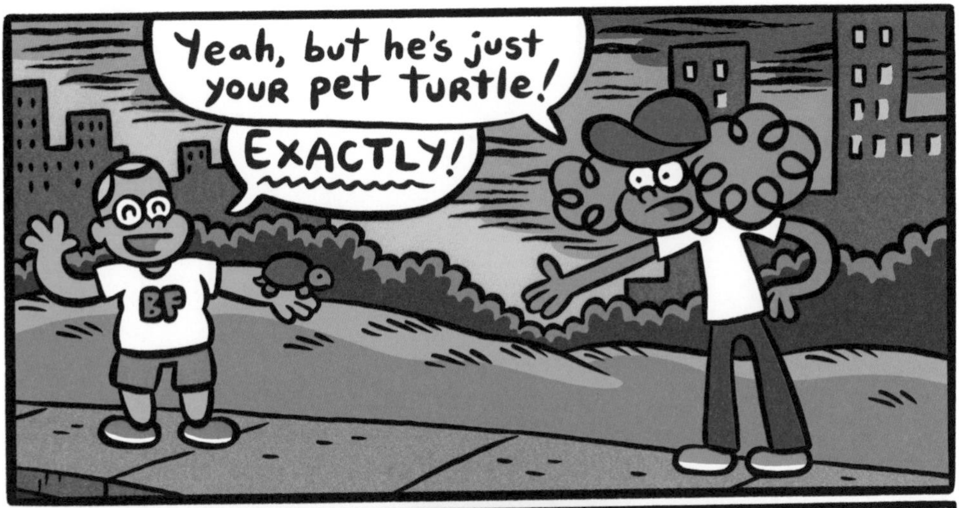
Yeah, but he's just your pet turtle!
EXACTLY!

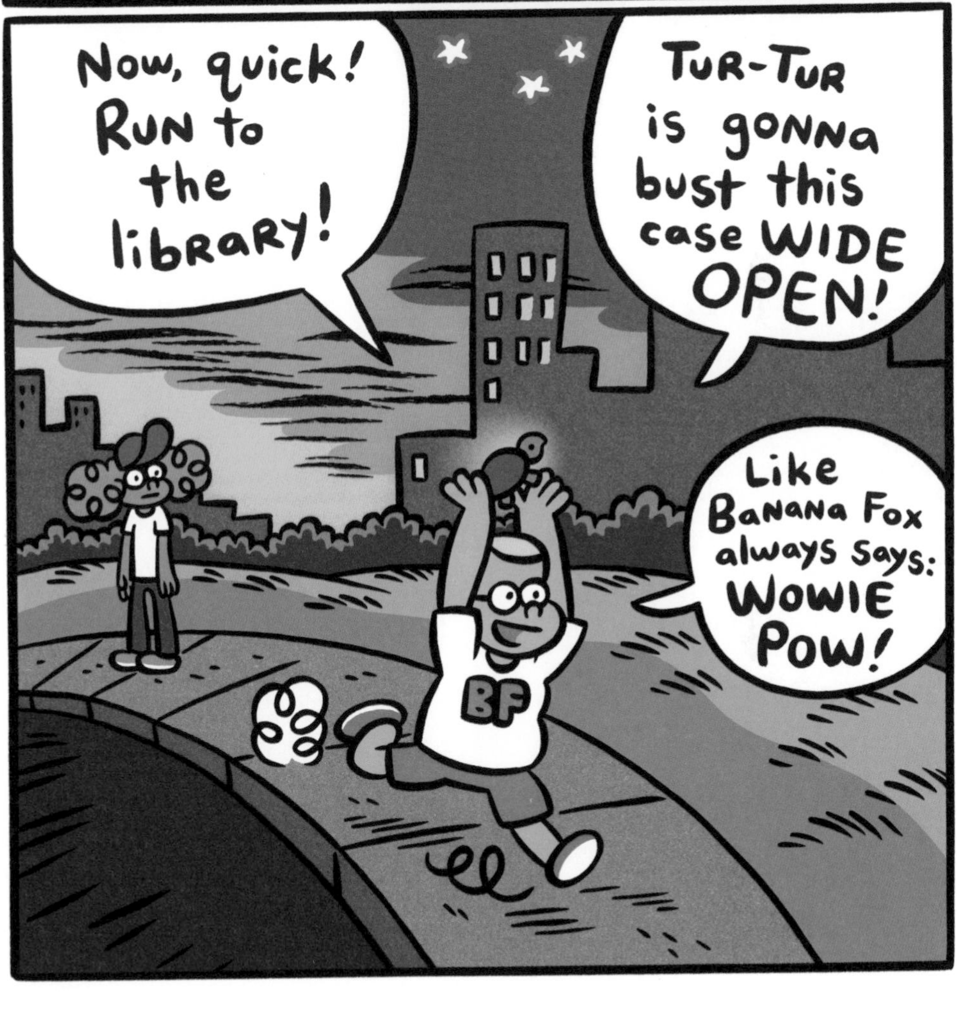
Now, quick! RUN to the library!
TUR-TUR is gonna bust this case WIDE OPEN!
Like Banana Fox always says: WOWIE POW!

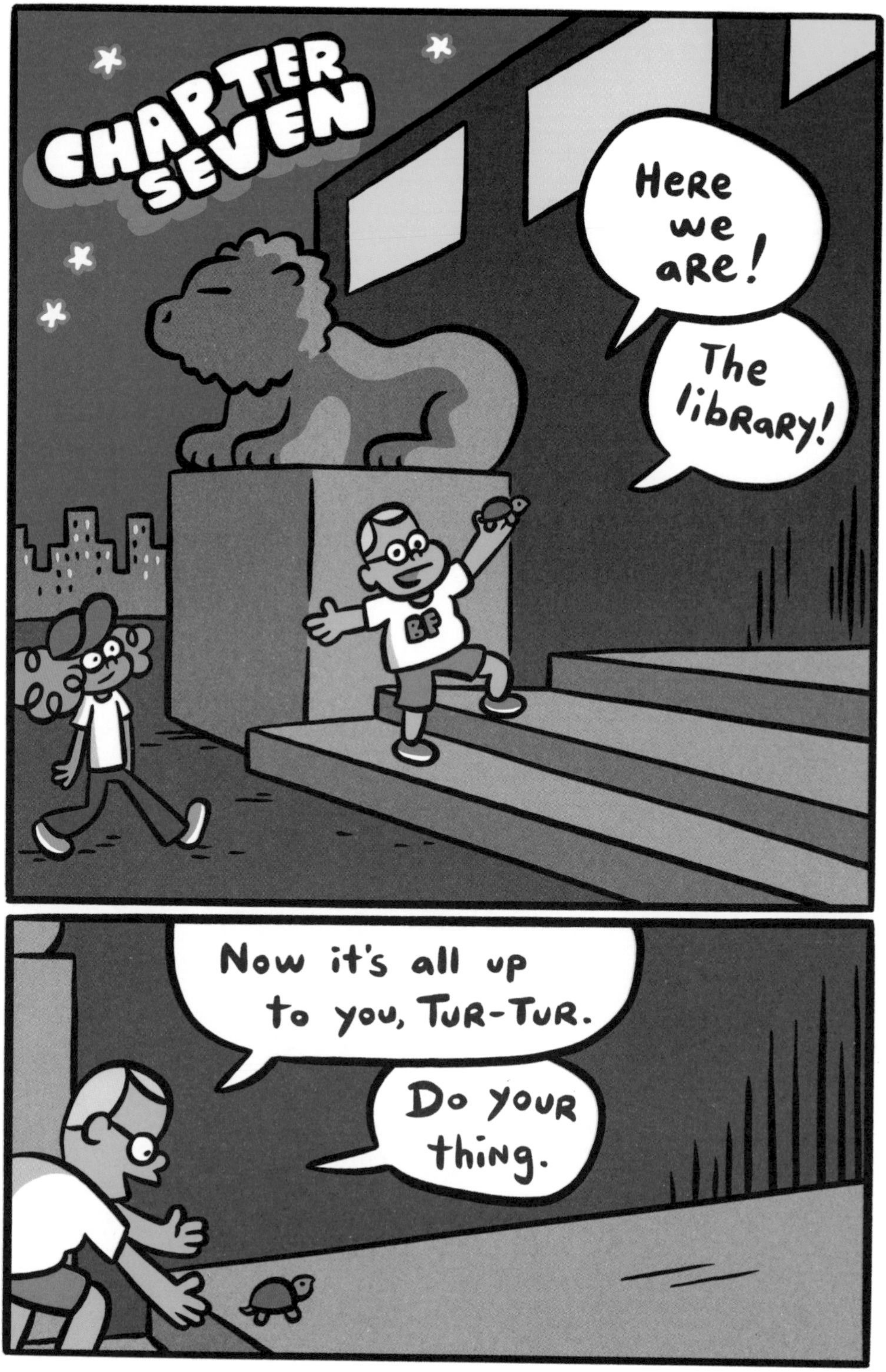
CHAPTER SEVEN
Here we are!
The library!
Now it's all up to you, TUR-TUR.
Do your thing.

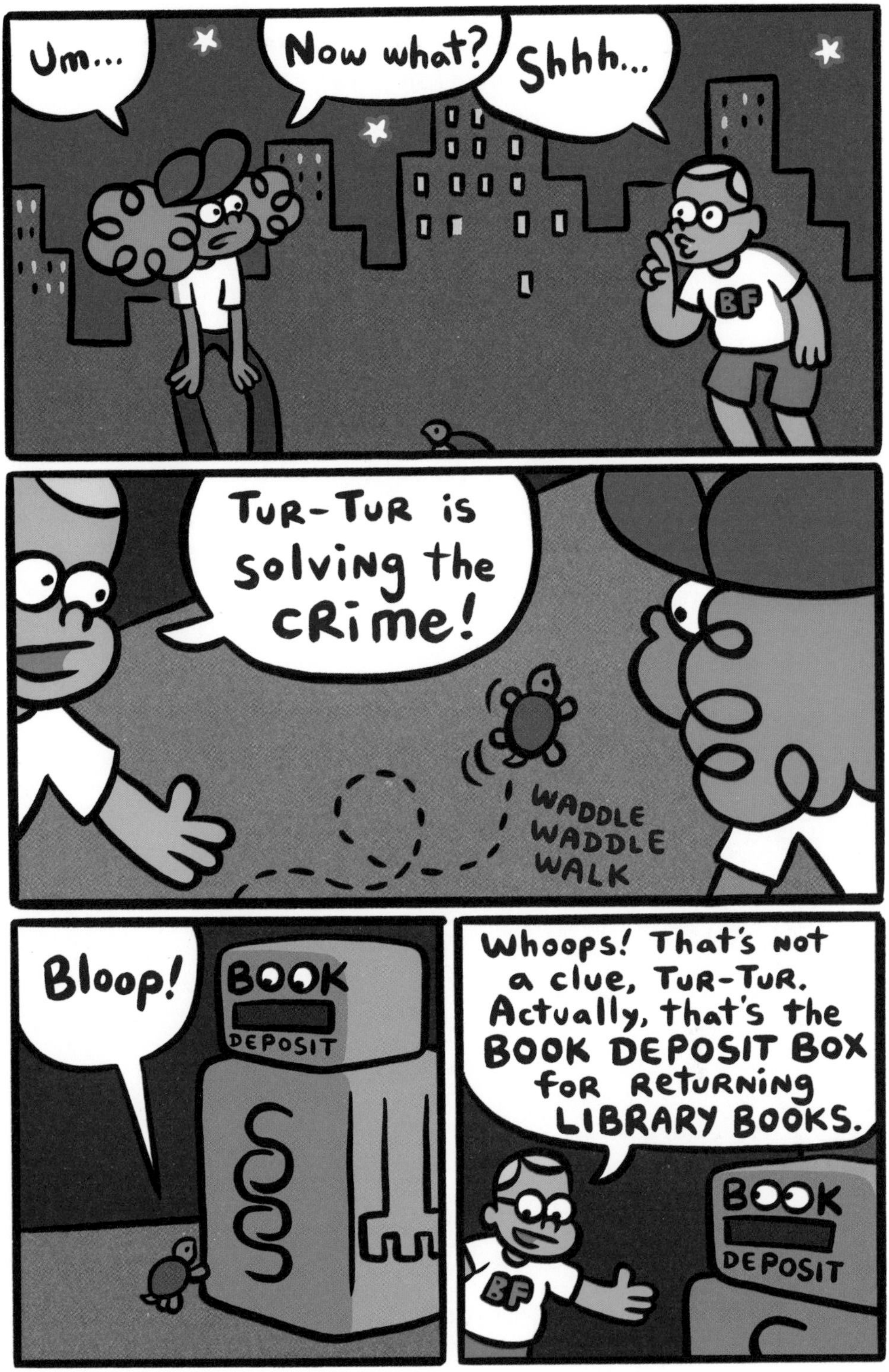
Um...
Now what?
Shhh...
TUR-TUR is solving the CRIME!
WADDLE
WADDLE
WALK
Bloop!
BOOK
DEPOSIT
Whoops! That's not a clue, TUR-TUR. Actually, that's the BOOK DEPOSIT BOX for RETURNING LIBRARY BOOKS.
BOOK
DEPOSIT

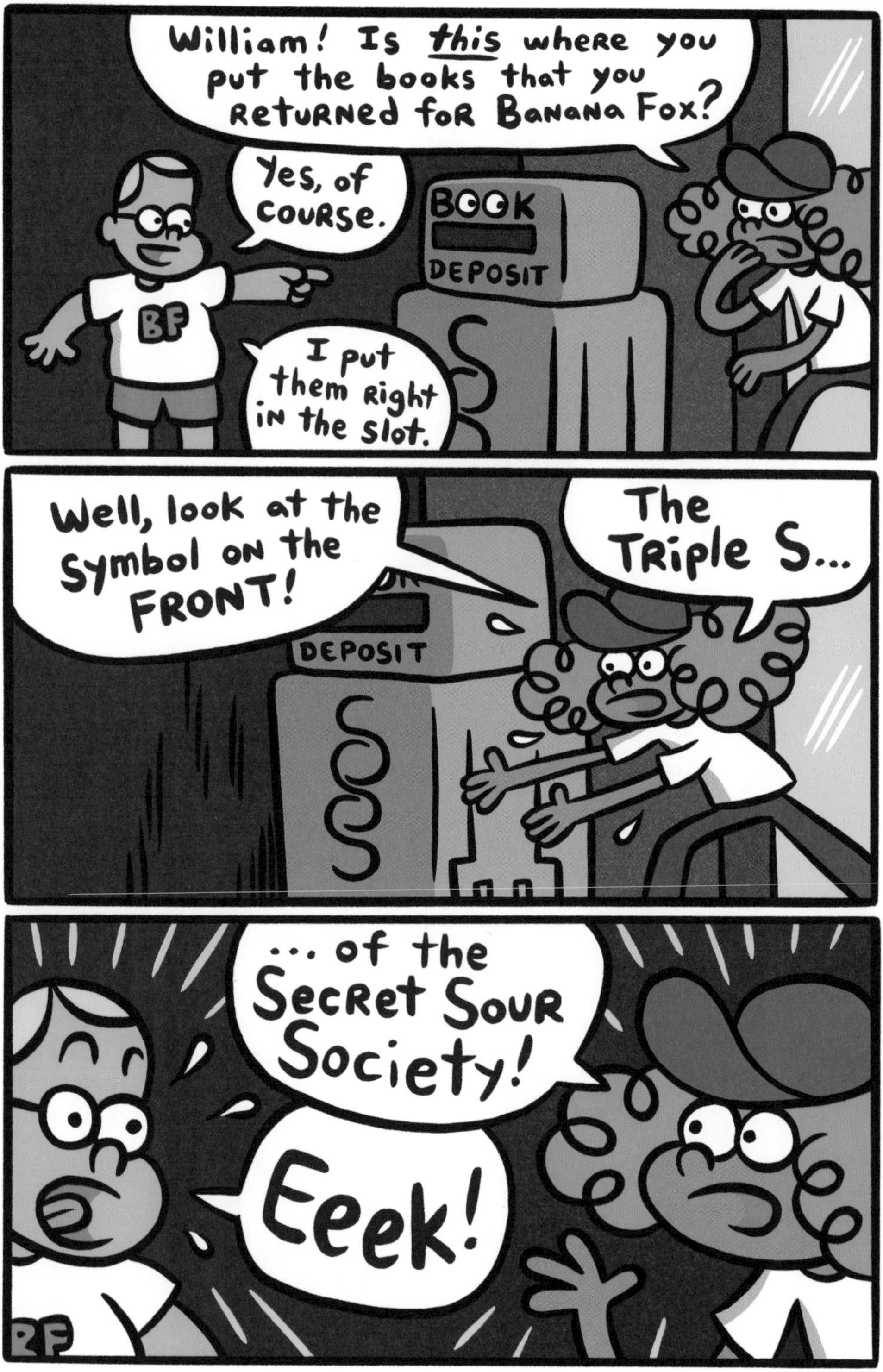
William! Is this where you put the books that you returned for Banana Fox?
Yes, of course.
BOOK DEPOSIT
BF
I put them right in the slot.
Well, look at the symbol on the FRONT!
The Triple S...
DEPOSIT
...of the Secret Sour Society!
Eeek!

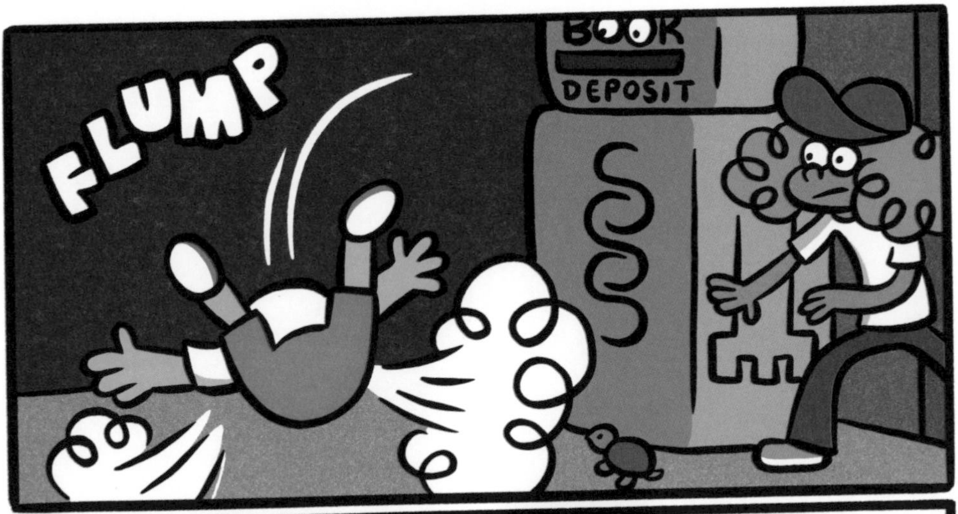
FLUMP
BOOK DEPOSIT

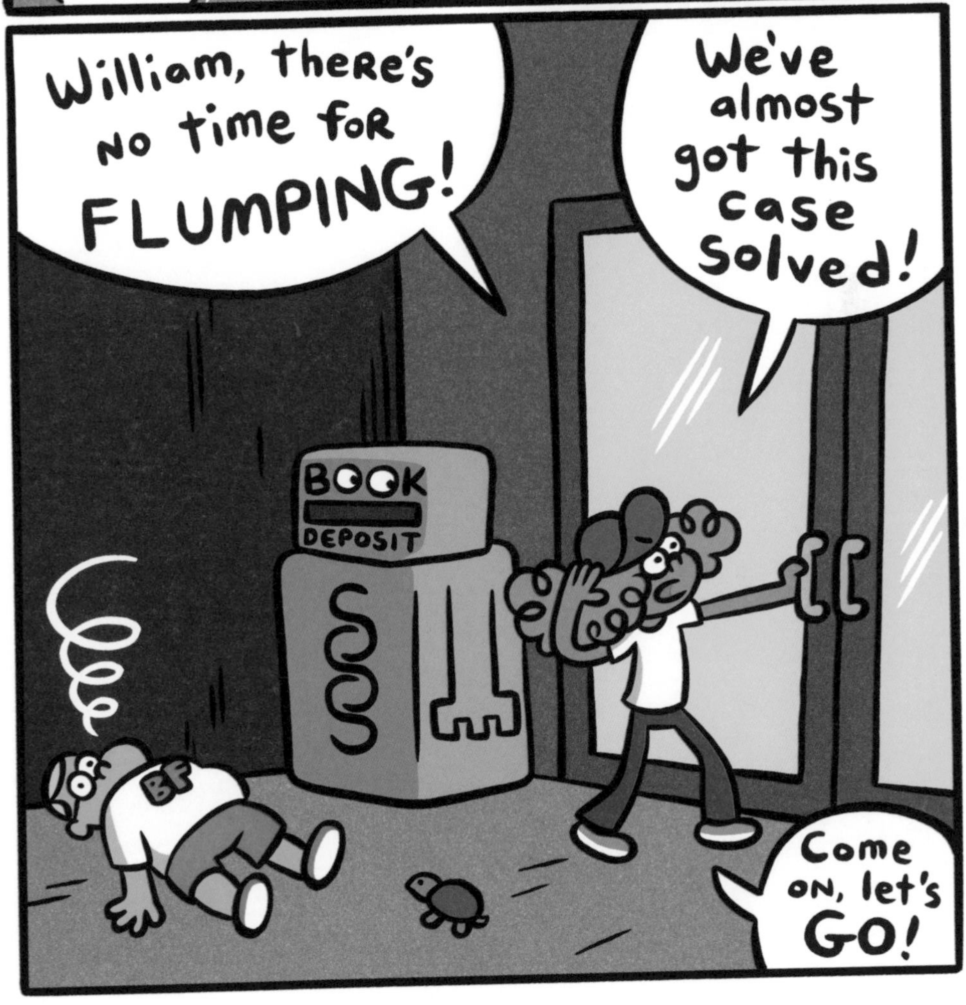
William, there's no time for FLUMPING!
We've almost got this case solved!
BOOK DEPOSIT
BF
Come on, let's GO!

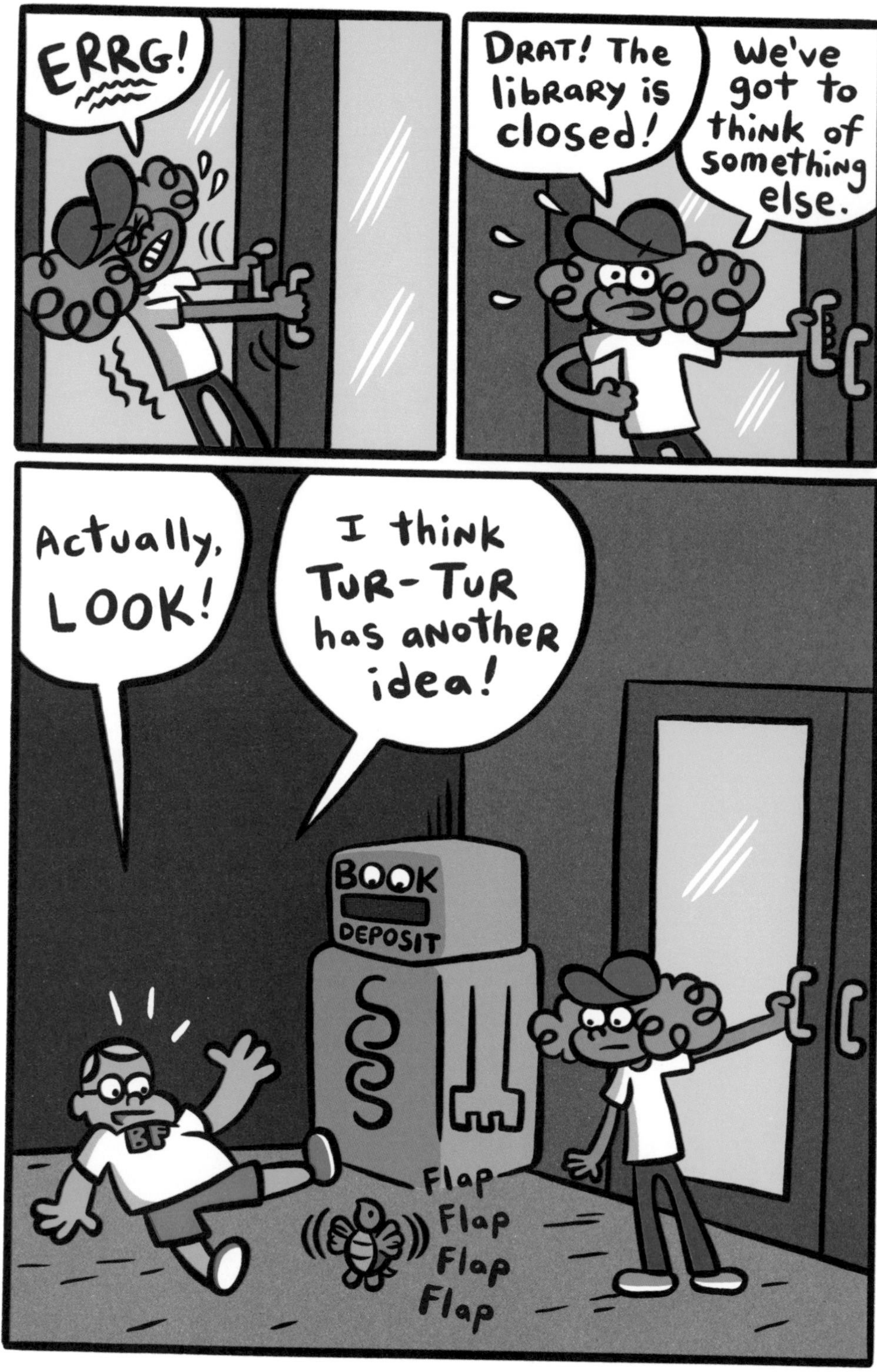
ERRG!
DRAT! The library is closed!
We've got to think of something else.
Actually, LOOK!
I think TUR-TUR has another idea!
BOOK DEPOSIT
BF
Flap Flap Flap Flap

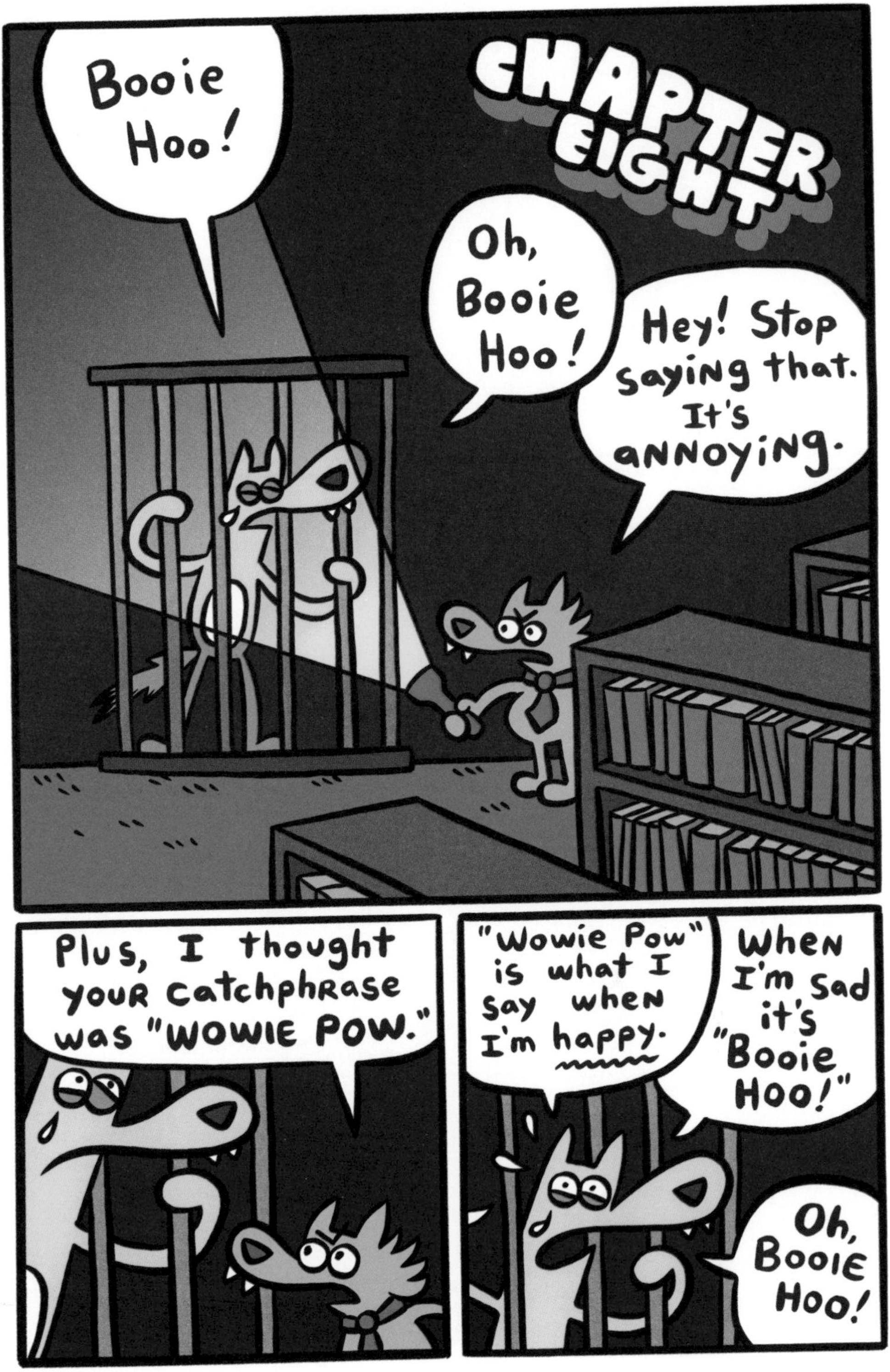
CHAPTER EIGHT
Booie Hoo!
Oh, Booie Hoo!
Hey! Stop saying that. It's annoying.
Plus, I thought your catchphrase was "WOWIE POW."
"Wowie Pow" is what I say when I'm happy.
When I'm sad it's "Booie Hoo!"
Oh, Booie Hoo!

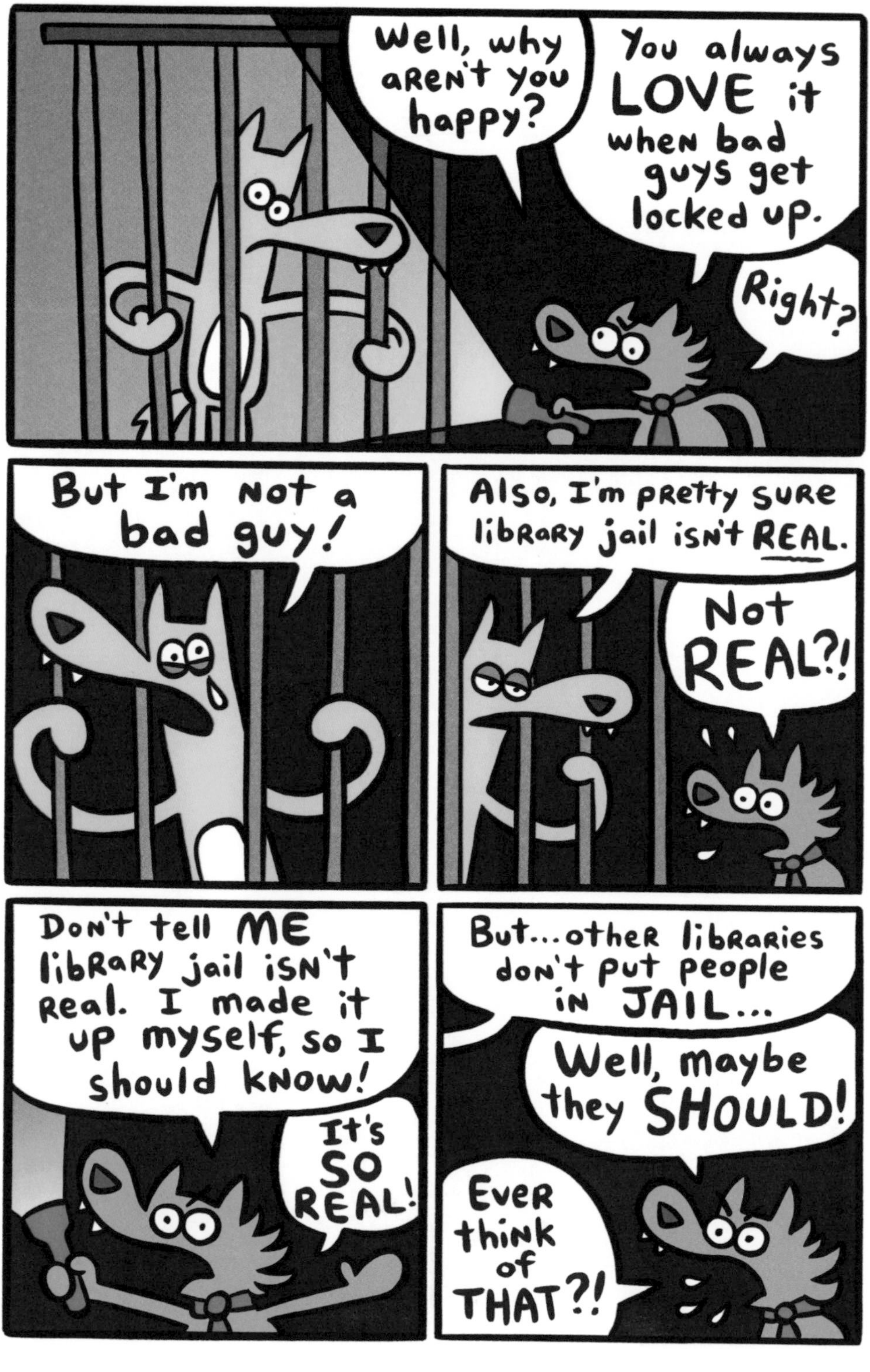
Well, why aren't you happy?
You always LOVE it when bad guys get locked up.
Right?
But I'm not a bad guy!
Also, I'm pretty sure library jail isn't REAL.
Not REAL?!
Don't tell ME library jail isn't real. I made it up myself, so I should know!
It's SO REAL!
But...other libraries don't put people in JAIL...
Well, maybe they SHOULD!
Ever think of THAT?!

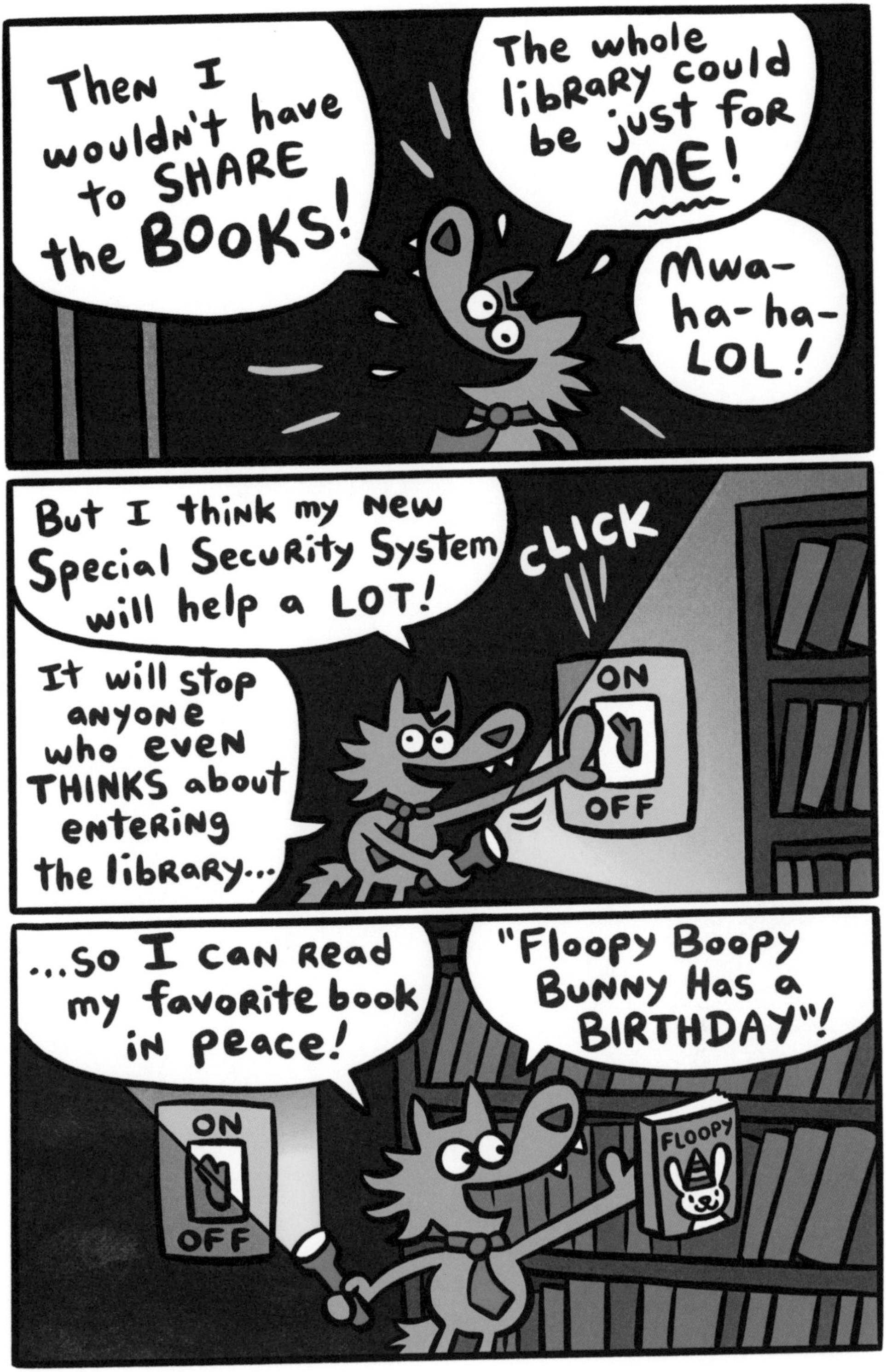
Then I wouldn't have to SHARE the BOOKS!
The whole library could be just for ME!
Mwa-ha-ha-LOL!
But I think my new Special Security System will help a LOT!
CLICK
ON
OFF
It will stop anyone who even THINKS about entering the library...
...So I can read my favorite book in peace!
"Floopy Boopy Bunny Has a BIRTHDAY"!
ON
OFF
FLOOPY

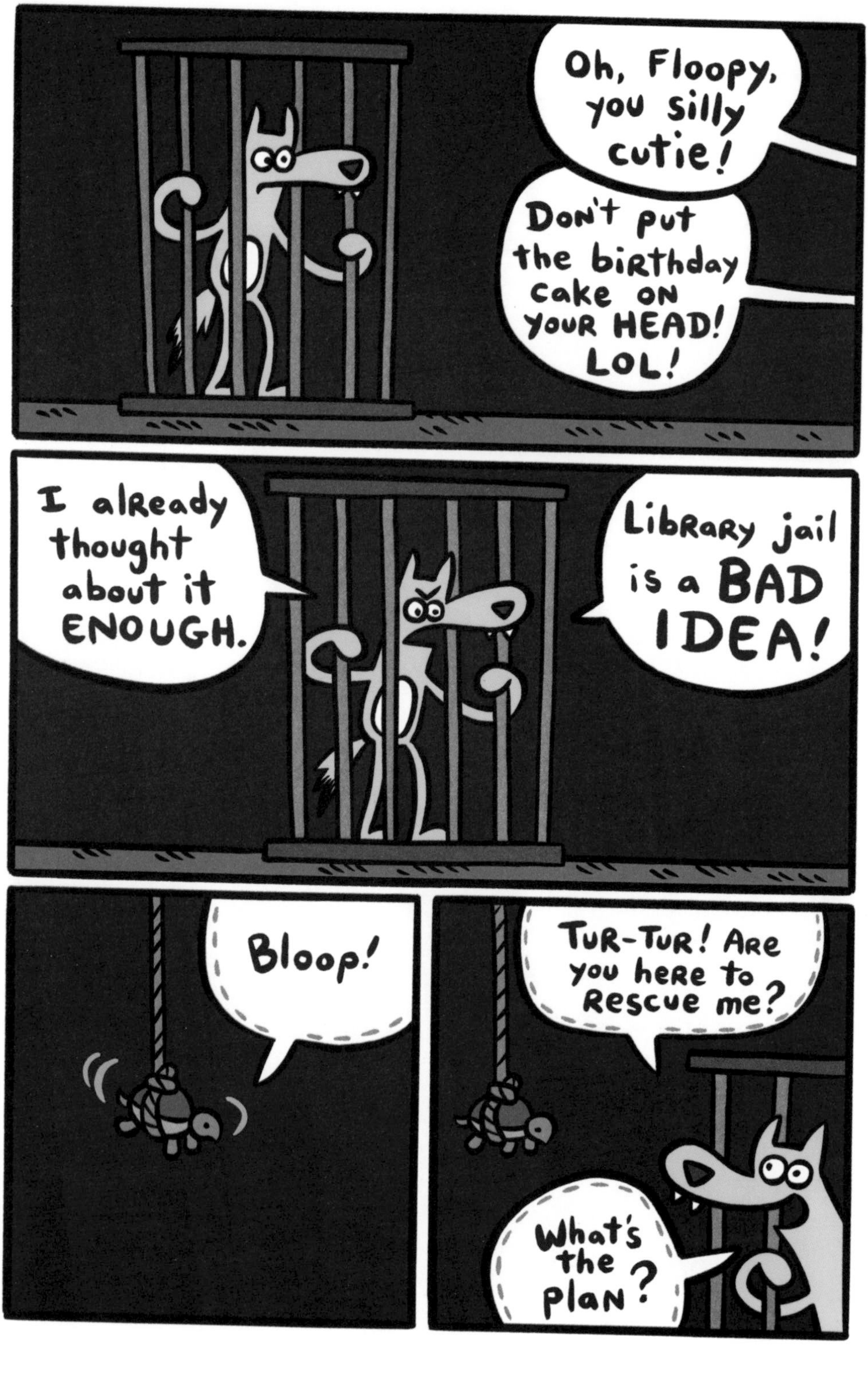
Oh, Floopy, you silly cutie!
Don't put the birthday cake ON YOUR HEAD! LOL!
I already thought about it ENOUGH.
Library jail is a BAD IDEA!
Bloop!
TUR-TUR! Are you here to Rescue me?
What's the plan?

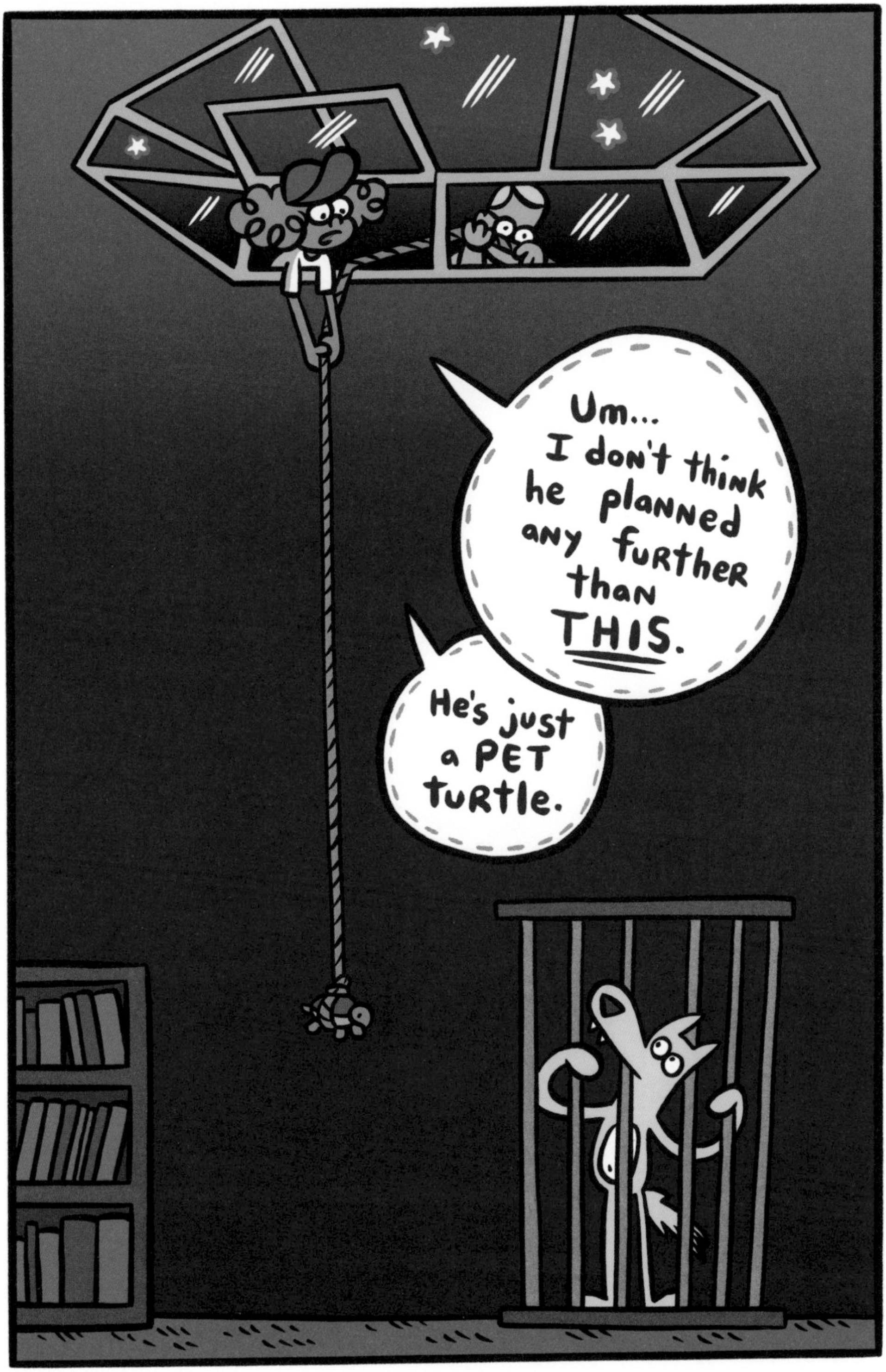
Um... I don't think he planned any further than THIS.
He's just a PET turtle.

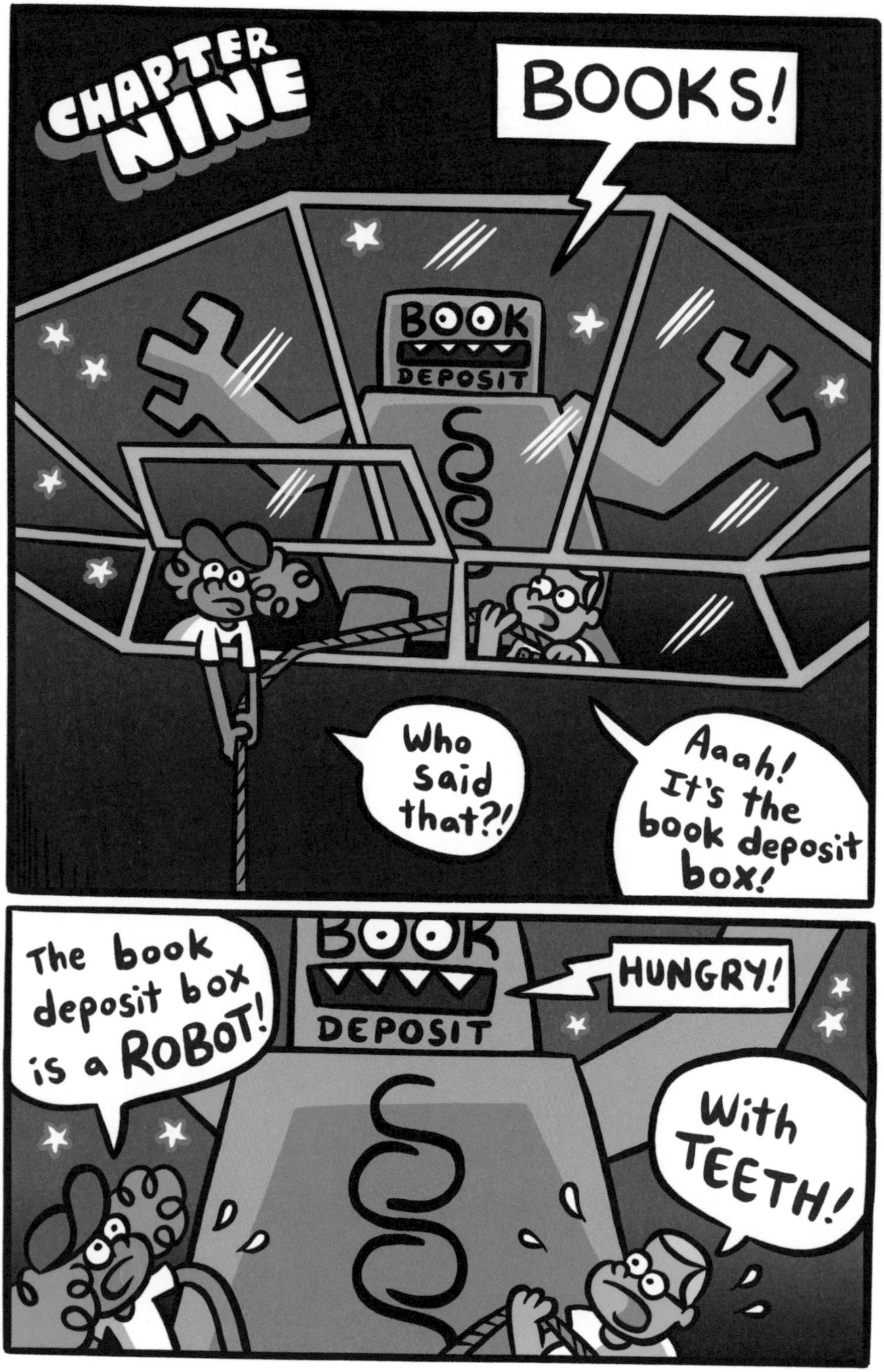
CHAPTER NINE
BOOKS!
BOOK DEPOSIT
Who said that?!
Aaah! It's the book deposit box!
BOOK DEPOSIT
The book deposit box is a ROBOT!
HUNGRY!
With TEETH!

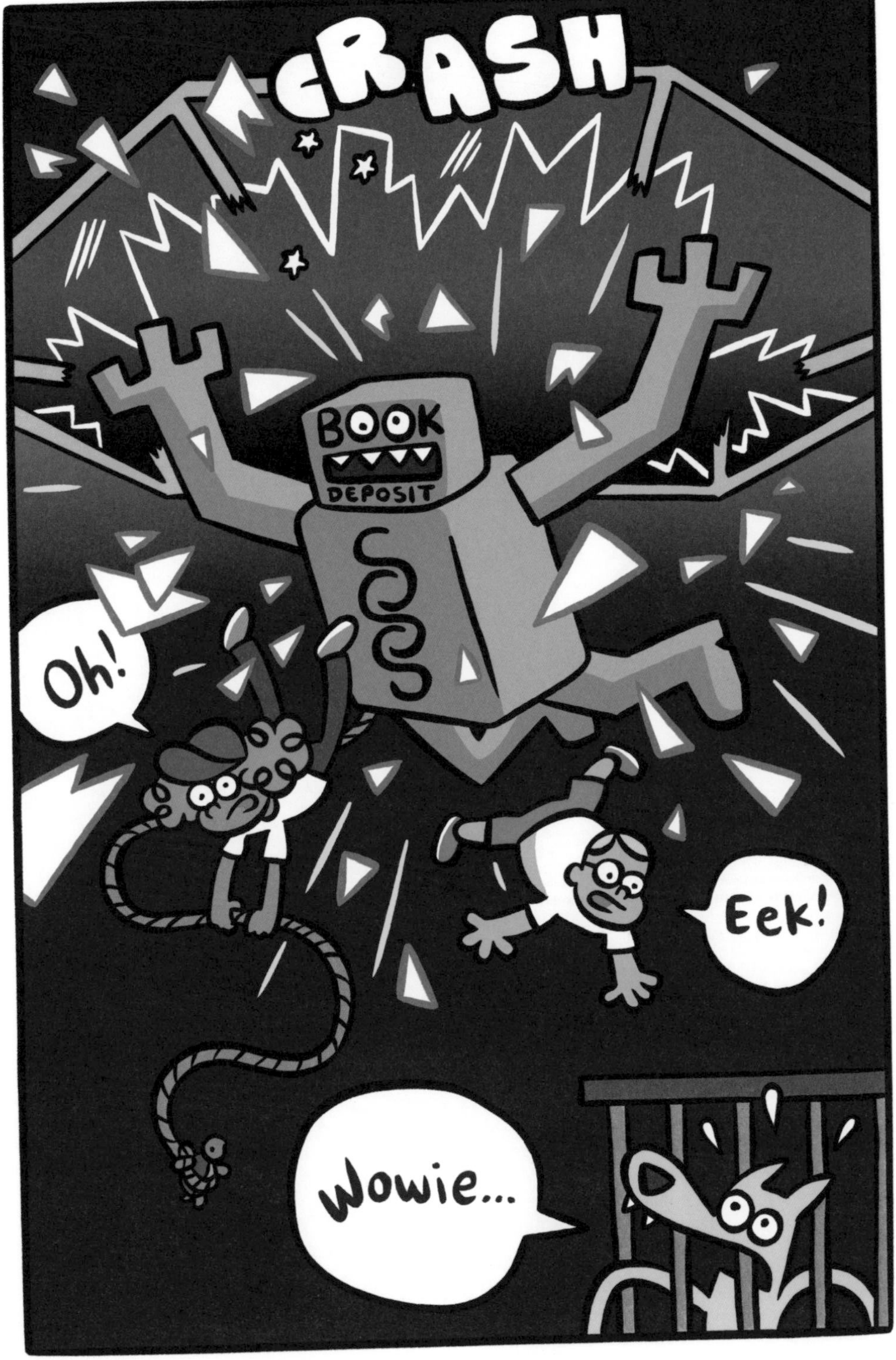
CRASH
BOOK DEPOSIT
Oh!
Eek!
Wowie...

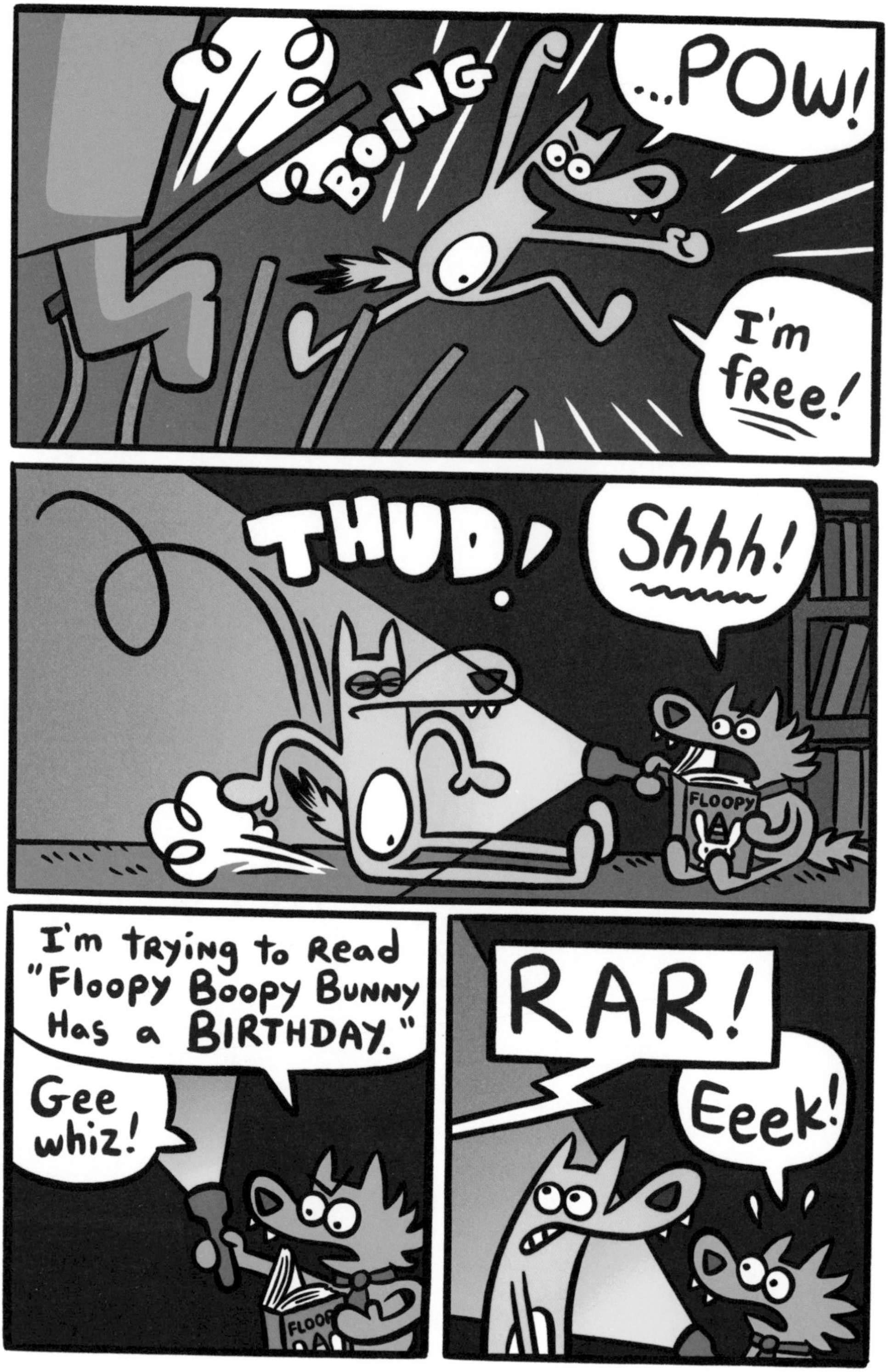
BOING
...POW!
I'm free!
THUD!
Shhh!
FLOOPY
I'm trying to Read "Floopy Boopy Bunny Has a BIRTHDAY."
Gee whiz!
RAR!
Eeek!

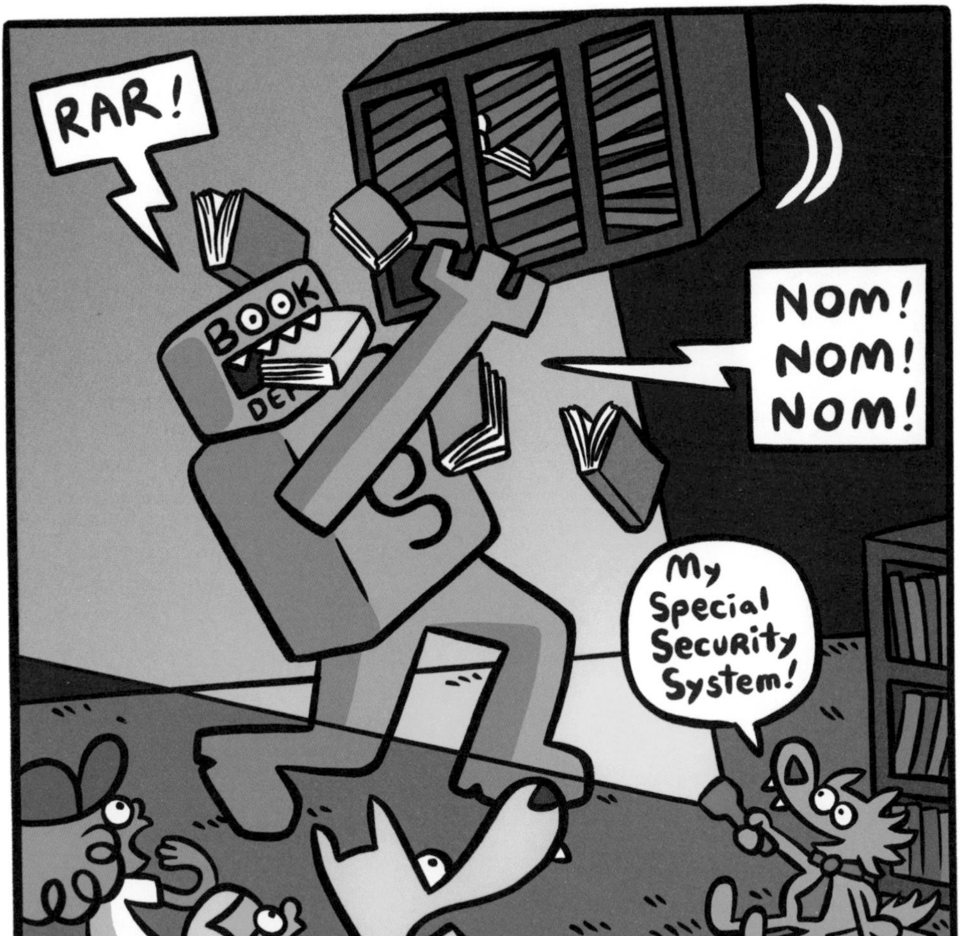
RAR!
NOM! NOM! NOM!
My Special Security System!

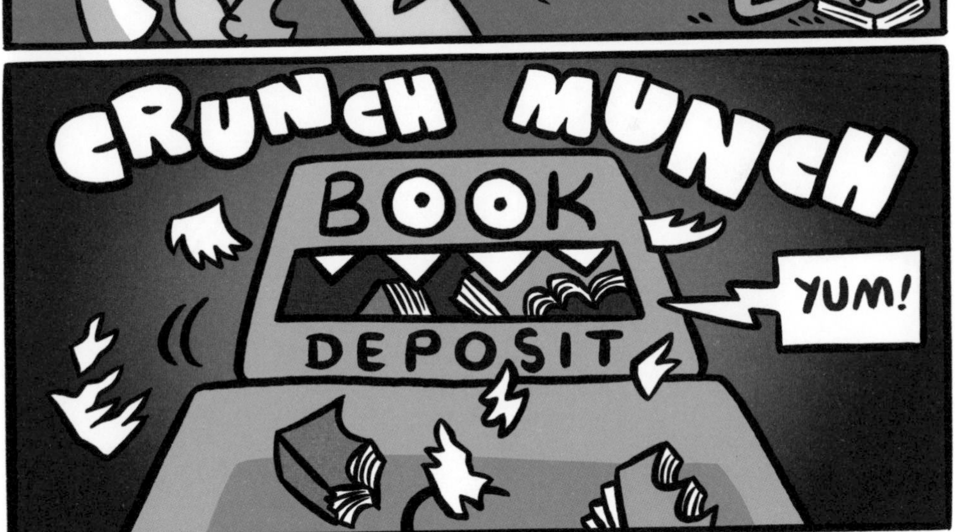
CRUNCH MUNCH
BOOK
DEPOSIT
YUM!

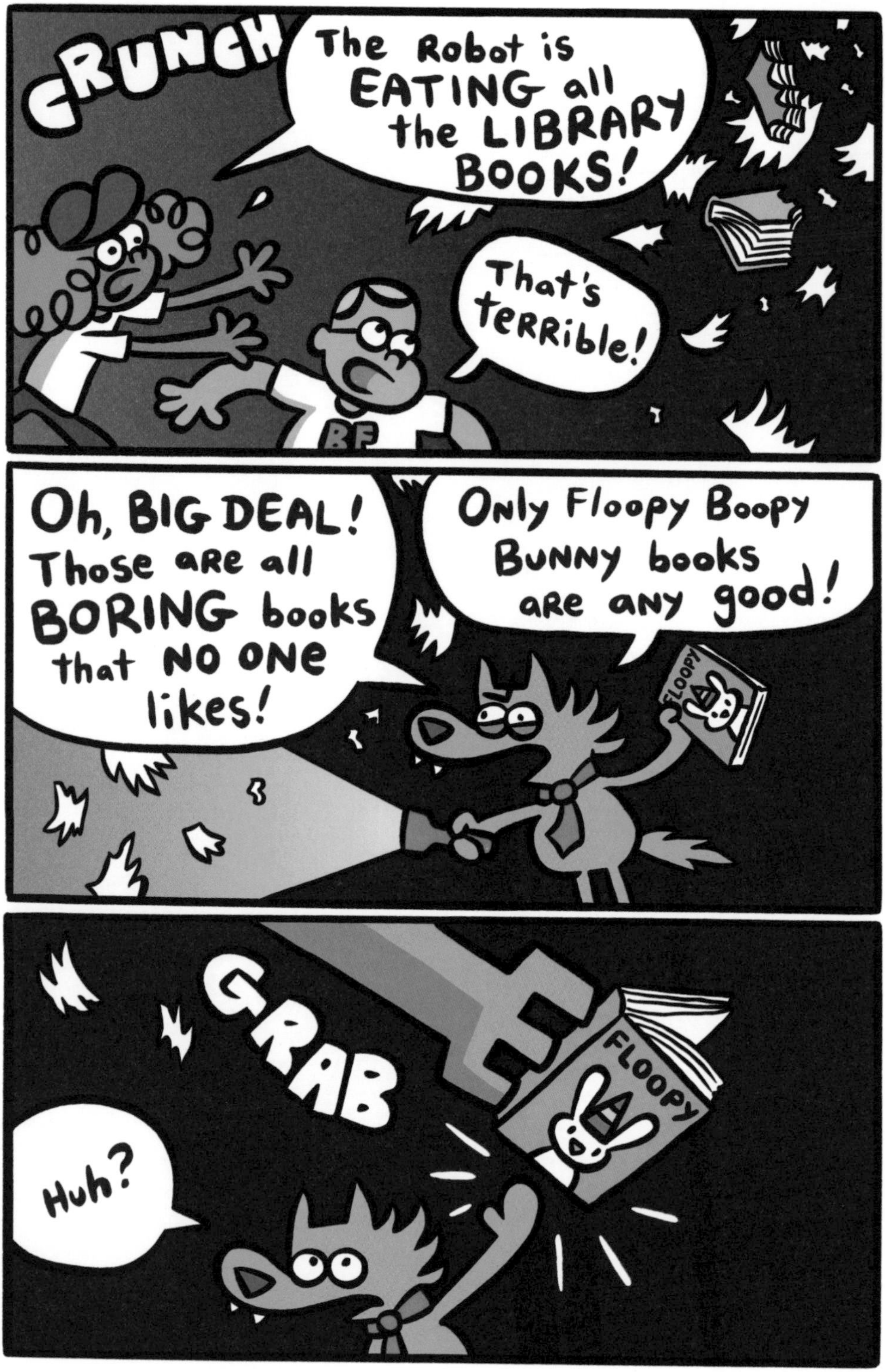

CRUNCH
The Robot is EATING all the LIBRARY BOOKS!
That's terrible!
BF
Oh, BIG DEAL! Those are all BORING books that NO ONE likes!
Only Floopy Boopy Bunny books are any good!
FLOOPY
GRAB
FLOOPY
Huh?

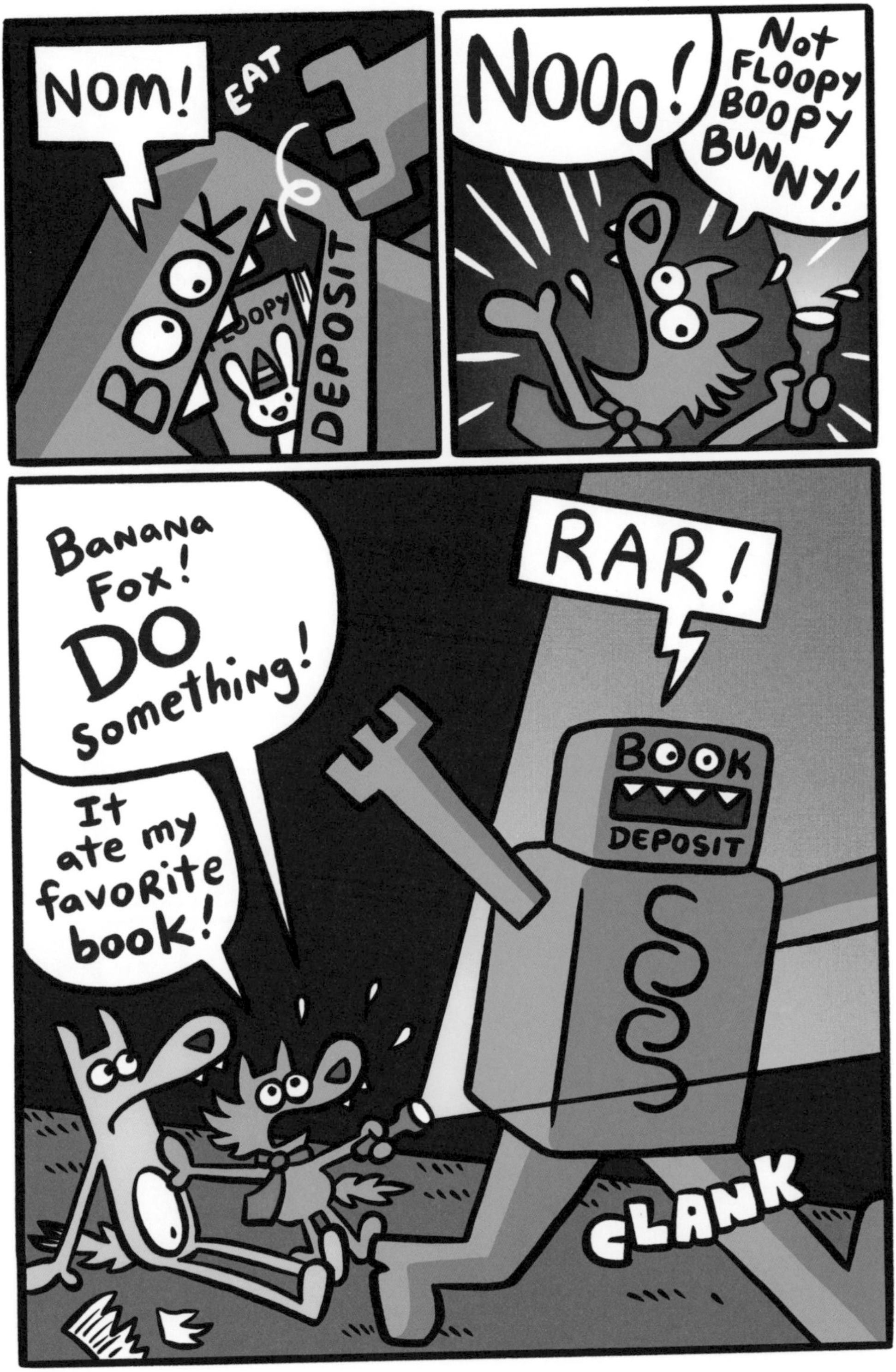
NOM!
EAT
BOOK
FLOOPY
DEPOSIT
NOOO!
Not FLOOPY BOOPY BUNNY!
Banana Fox! DO Something!
It ate my favorite book!
RAR!
BOOK
DEPOSIT
CLANK

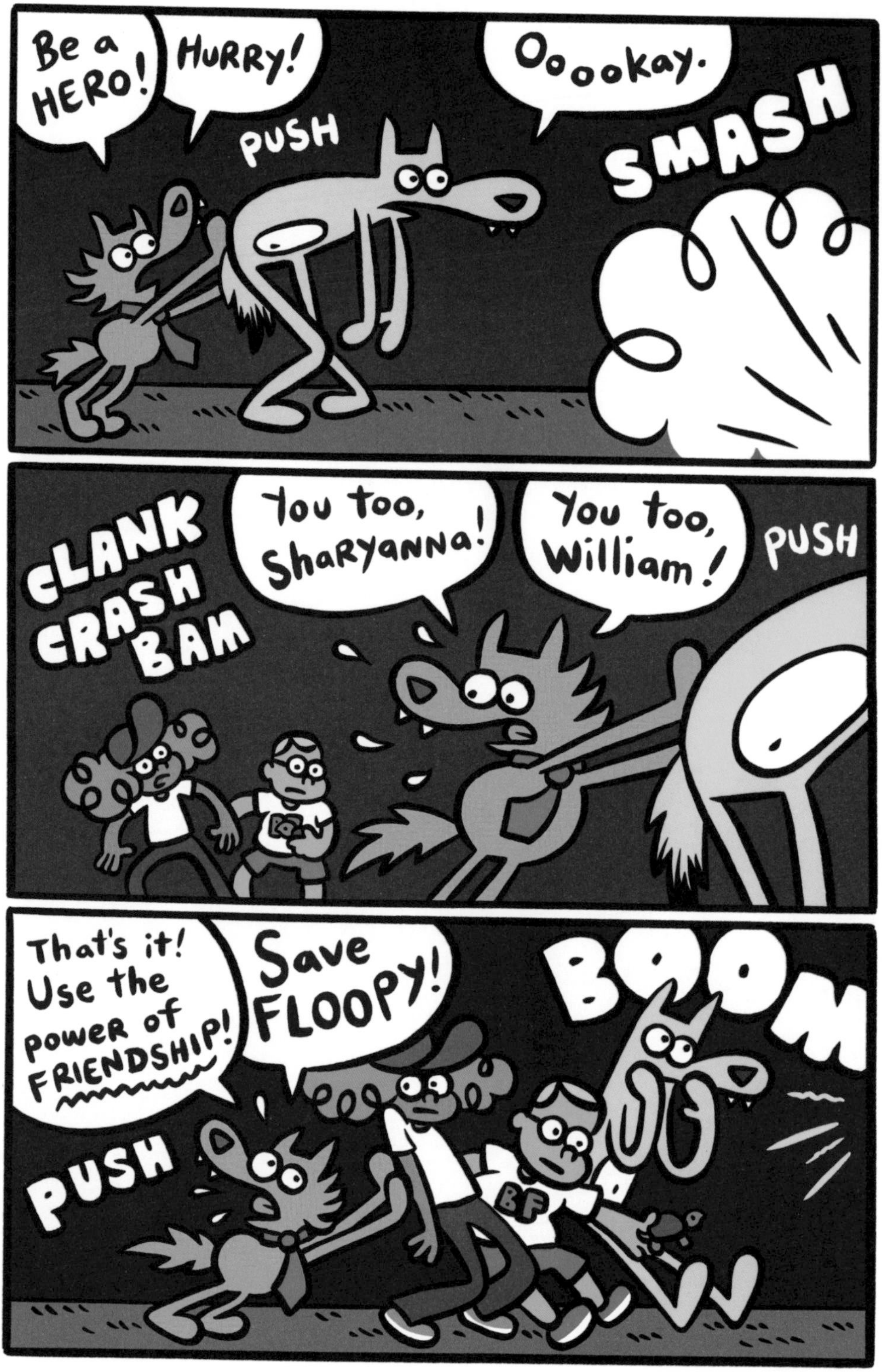

Be a HERO!
HURRY!
PUSH
Ooookay.
SMASH
CLANK
CRASH
BAM
You too, Sharyanna!
You too, William!
PUSH
That's it! Use the power of FRIENDSHIP!
Save FLOOPY!
BOOM
PUSH
BF

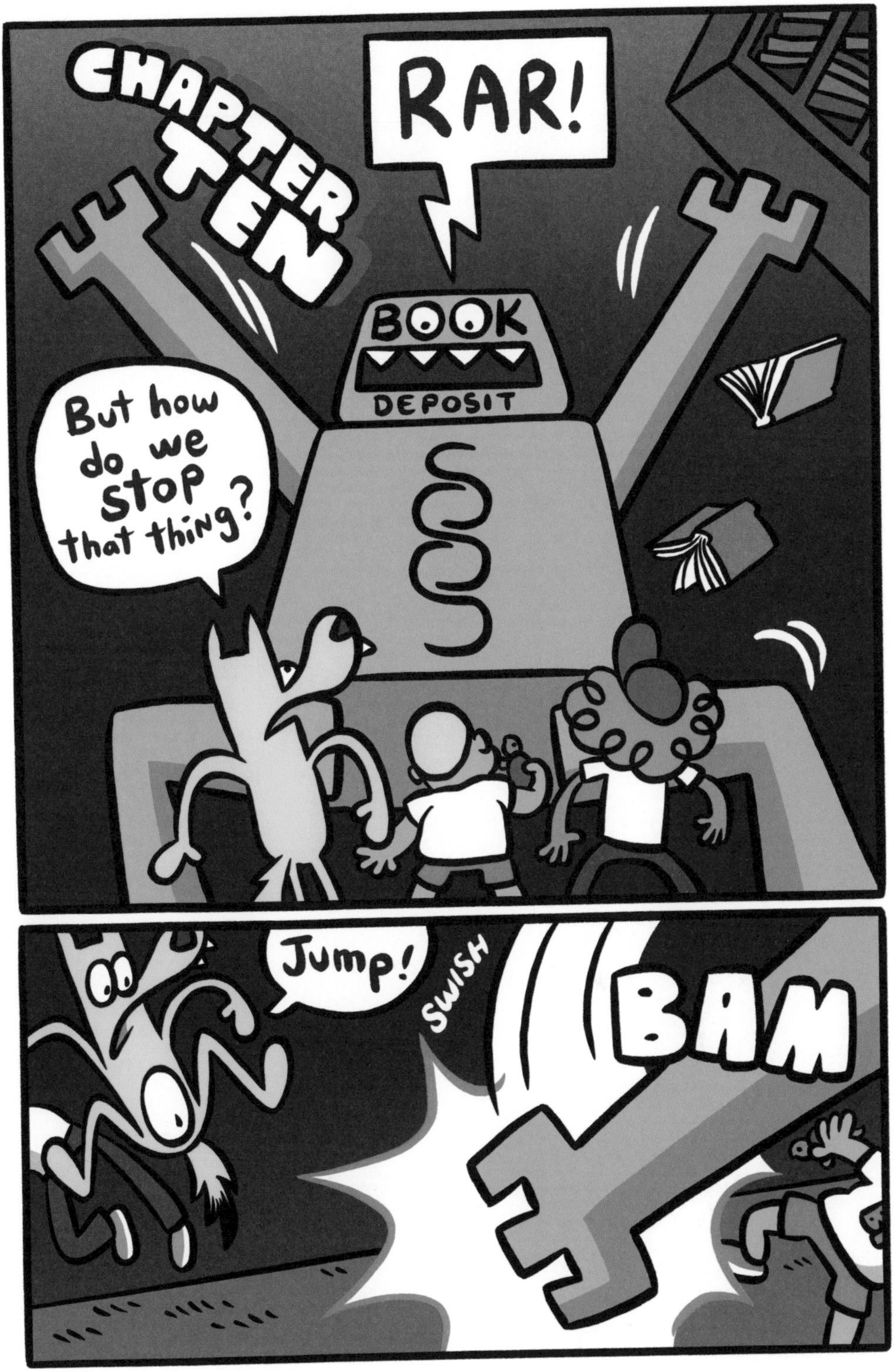

CHAPTER TEN
RAR!
BOOK
DEPOSIT
But how do we STOP that thing?
Jump!
SWISH
BAM

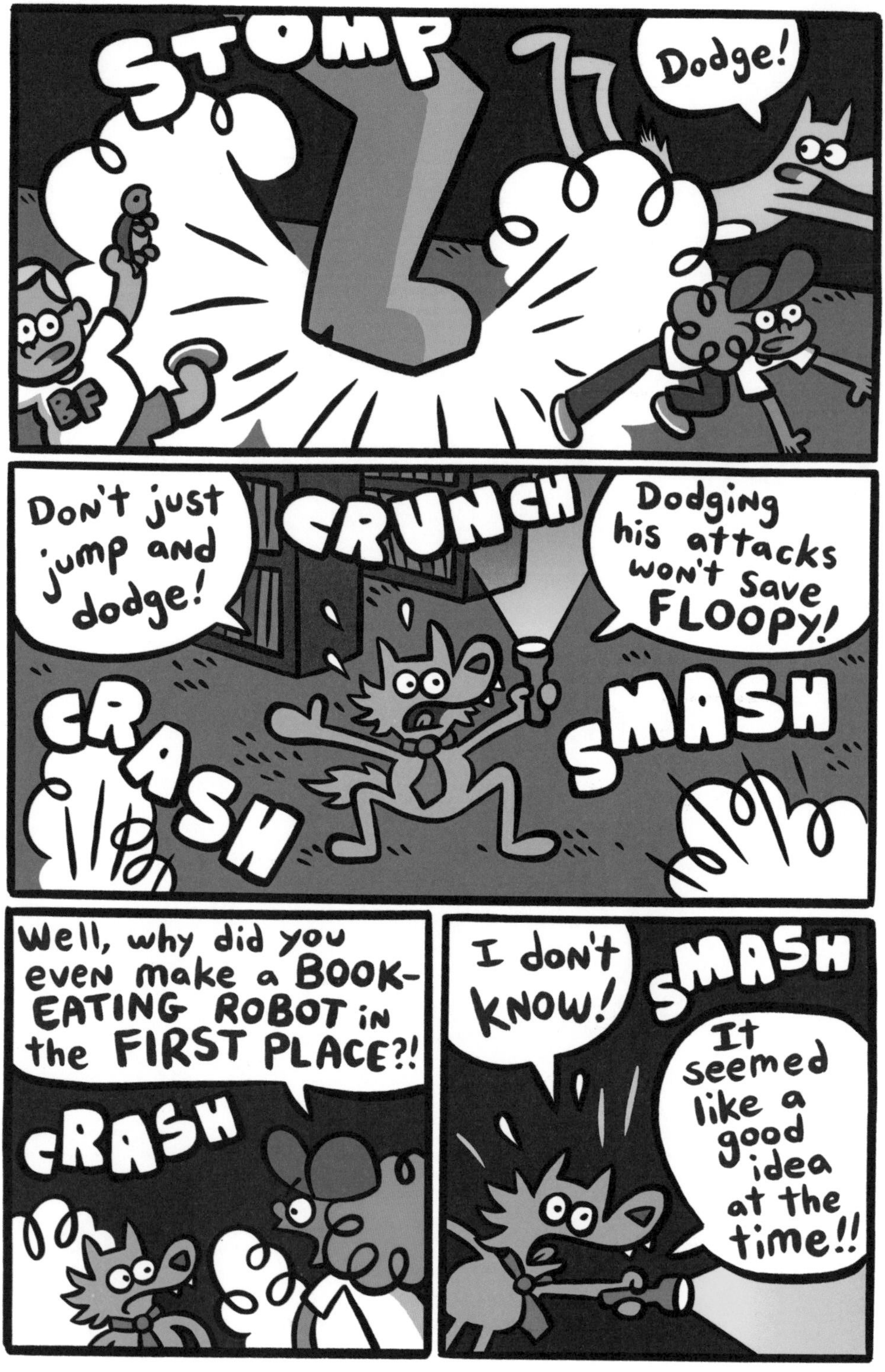
STOMP
Dodge!
Don't just jump and dodge!
CRUNCH
Dodging his attacks won't save FLOOPY!
CRASH
SMASH
Well, why did you even make a BOOK-EATING ROBOT in the FIRST PLACE?!
CRASH
I don't KNOW!
SMASH
It seemed like a good idea at the time!!

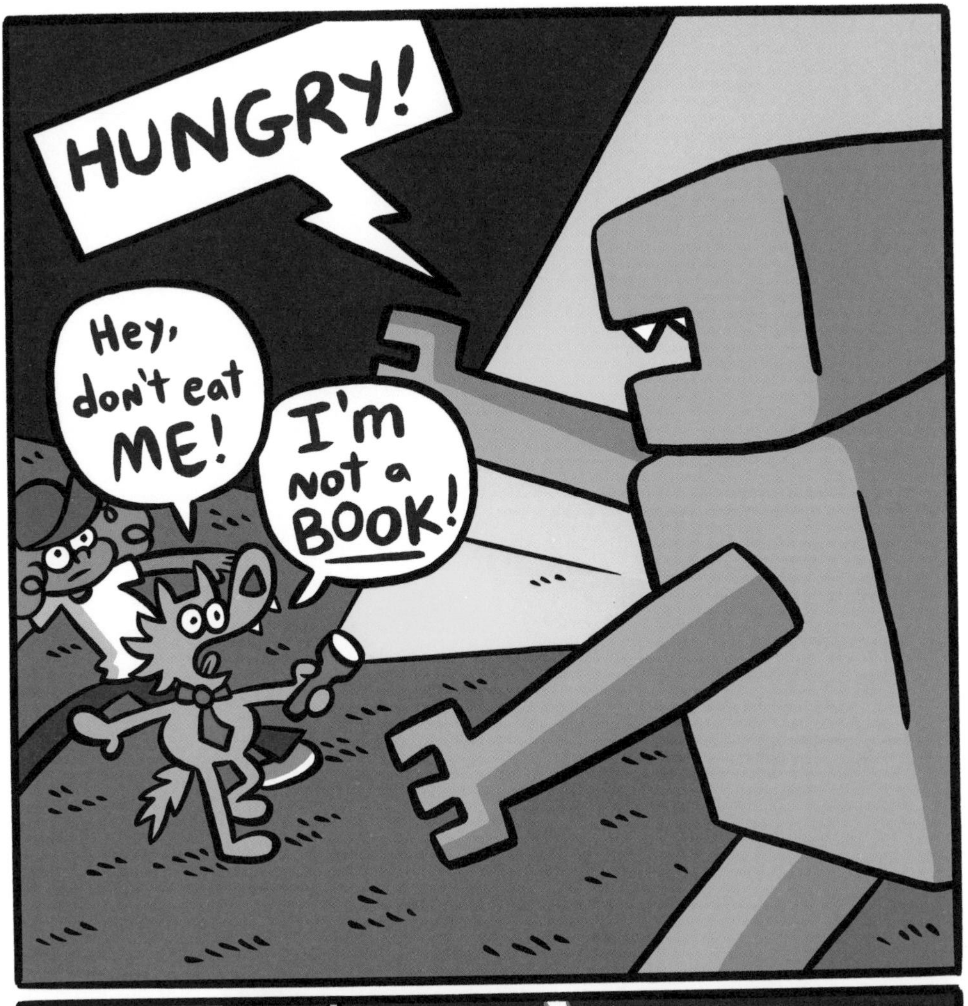
HUNGRY!
Hey, don't eat ME!
I'm not a BOOK!

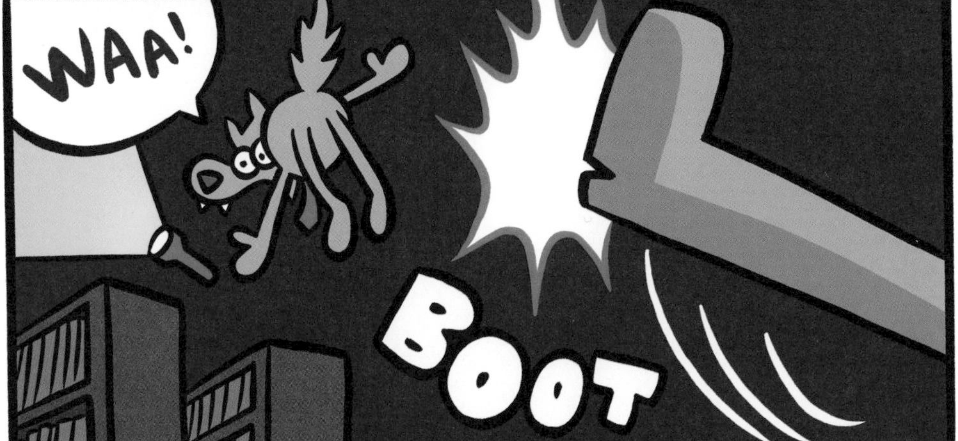
WAA!
BOOT

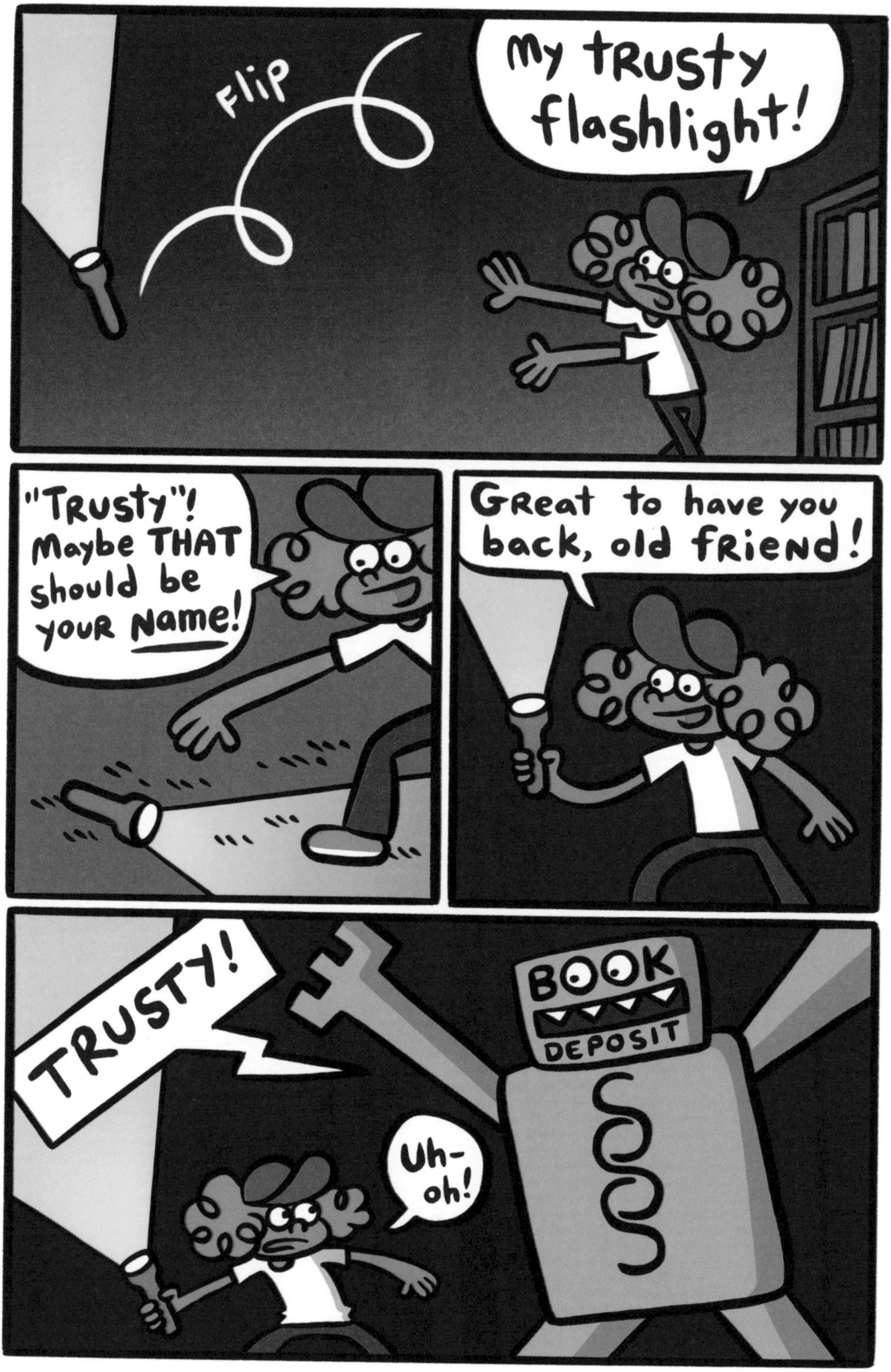
Flip
My trusty flashlight!
"Trusty"! Maybe THAT should be your Name!
Great to have you back, old friend!
TRUSTY!
BOOK DEPOSIT
Uh-oh!

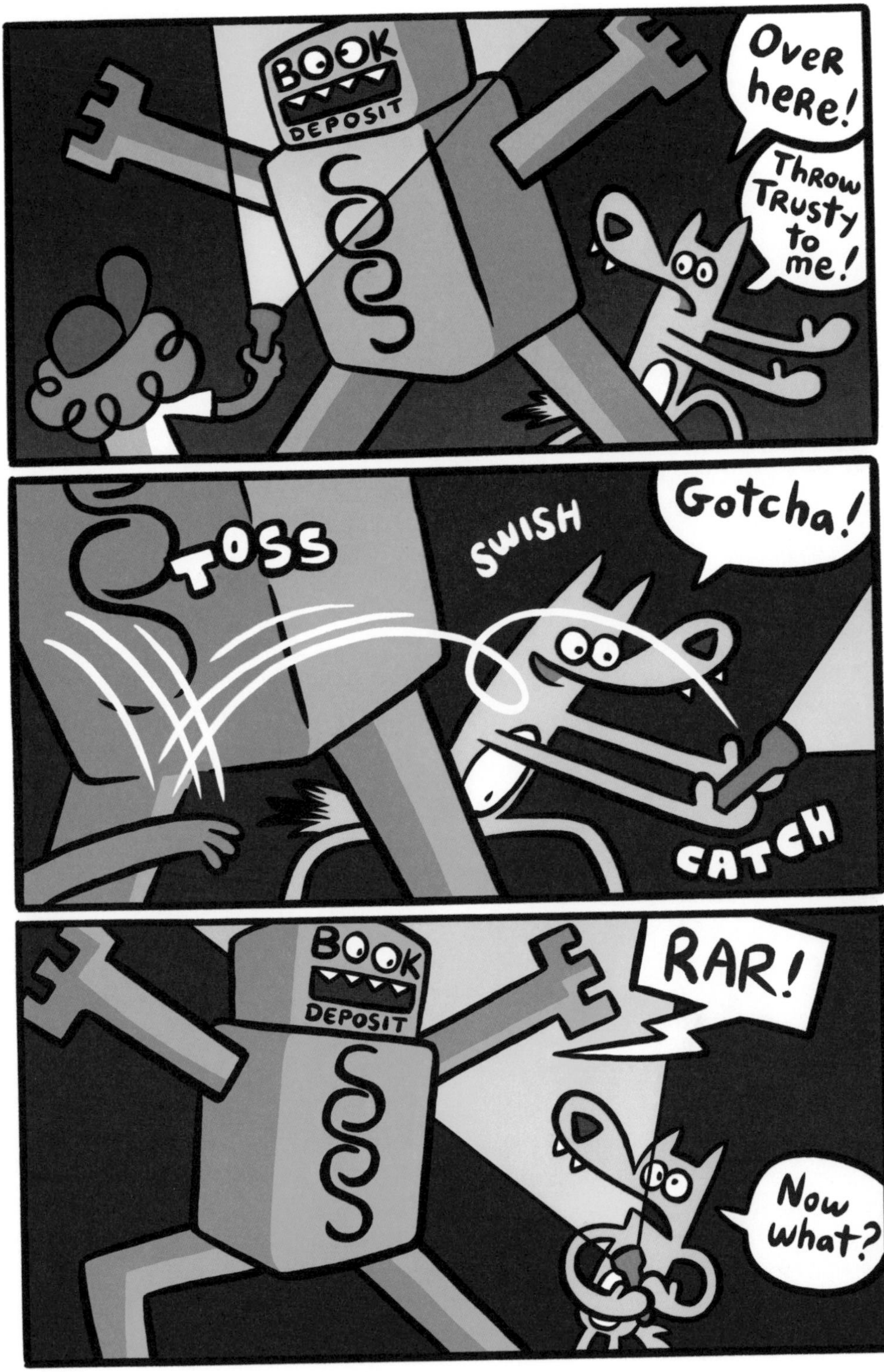
BOOK DEPOSIT
Over here!
Throw Trusty to me!
TOSS
SWISH
Gotcha!
CATCH
BOOK DEPOSIT
RAR!
Now what?

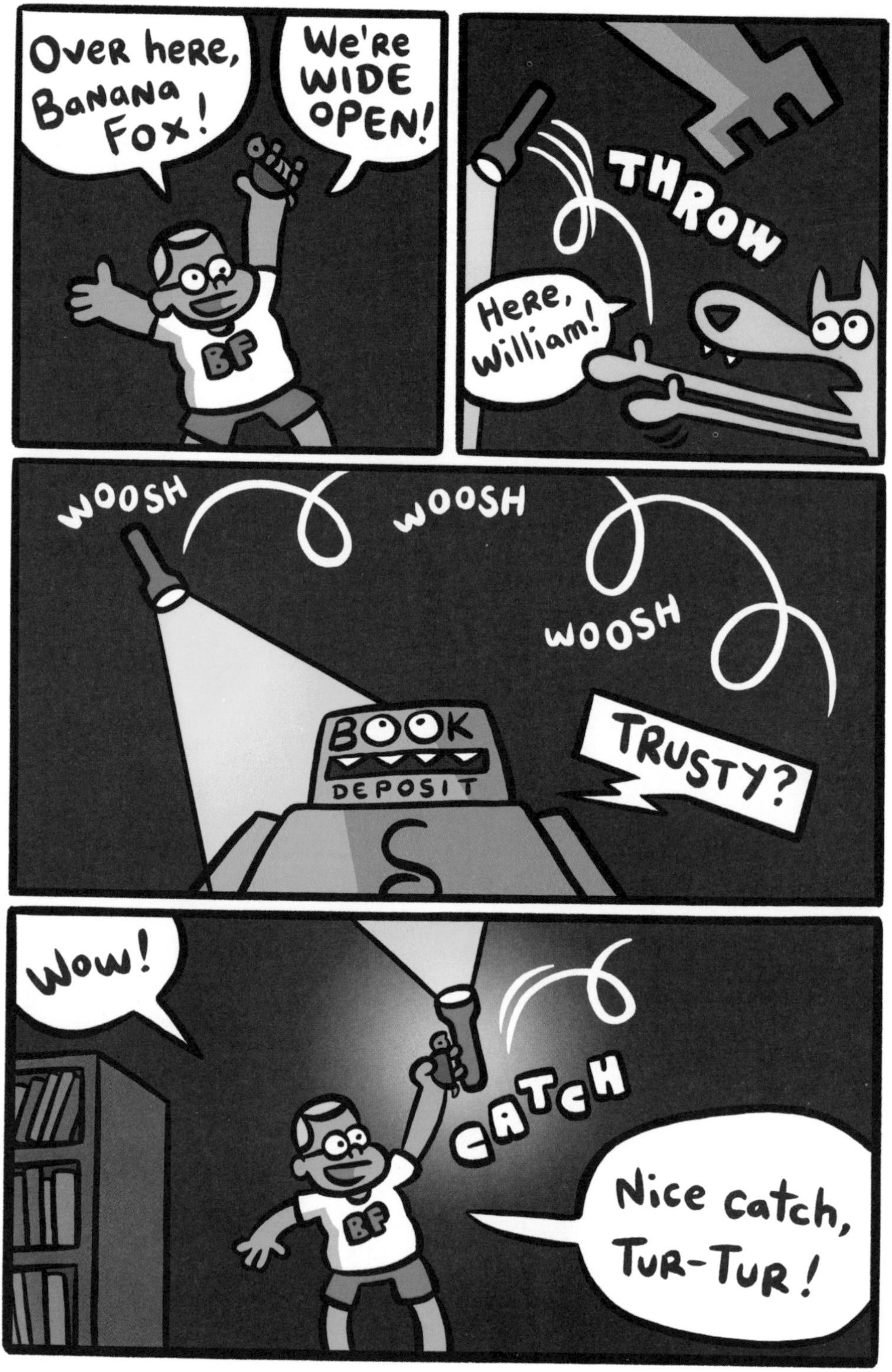
Over here, Banana Fox!
We're WIDE OPEN!
THROW
Here, William!
WOOSH
WOOSH
WOOSH
BOOK
DEPOSIT
TRUSTY?
Wow!
CATCH
Nice catch, Tur-Tur!

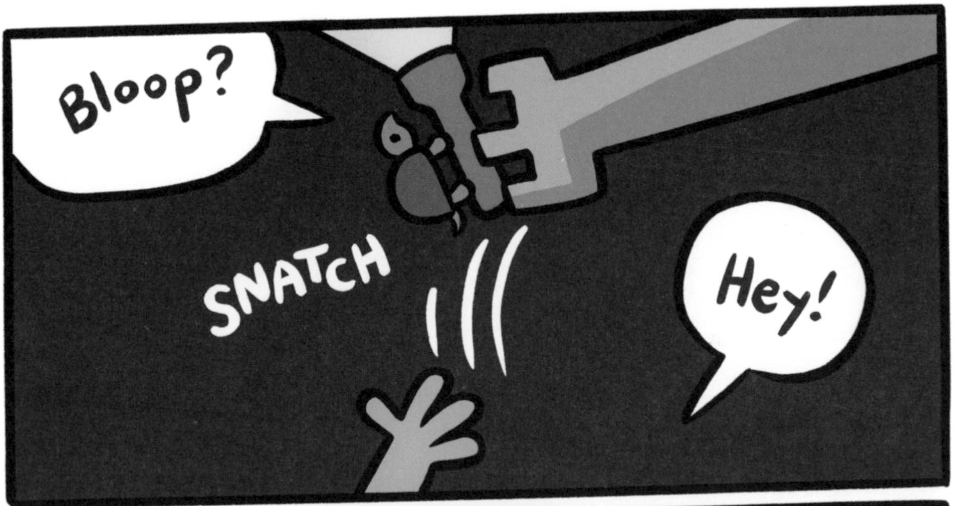
Bloop?
SNATCH
Hey!

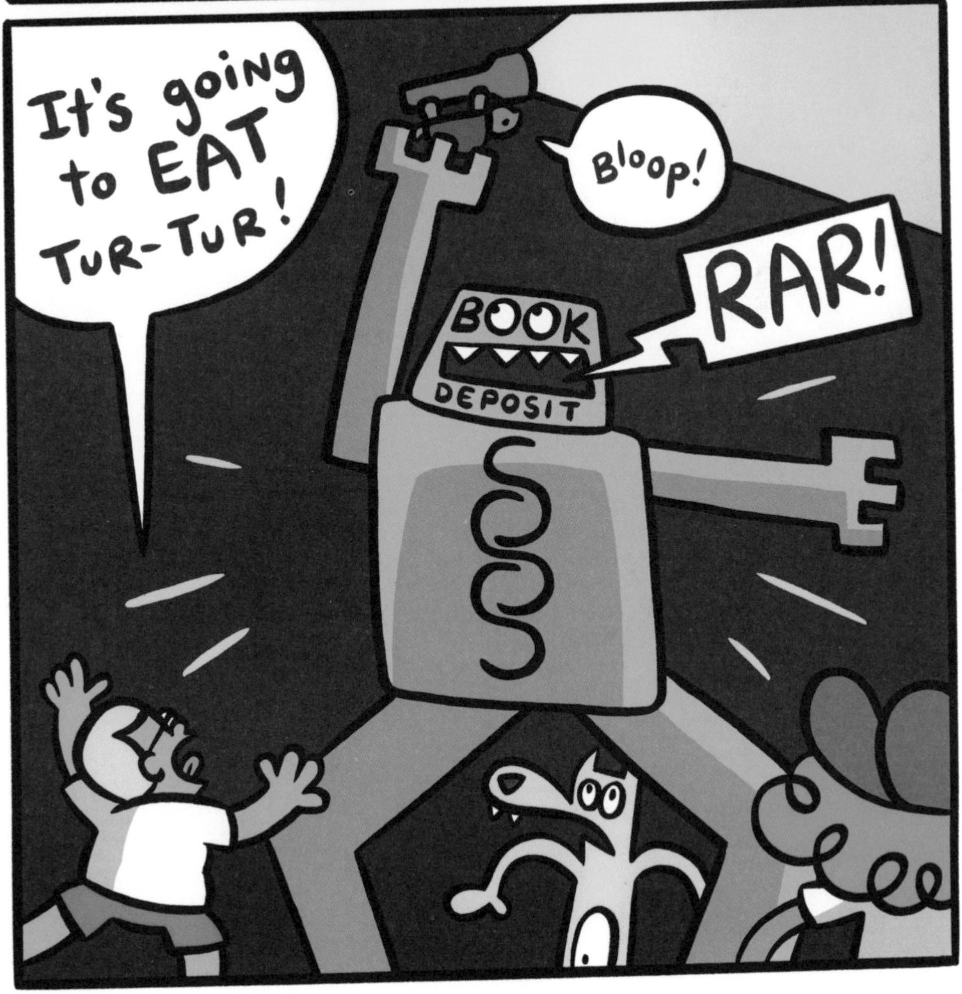
It's going to EAT TUR-TUR!
Bloop!
BOOK
DEPOSIT
RAR!

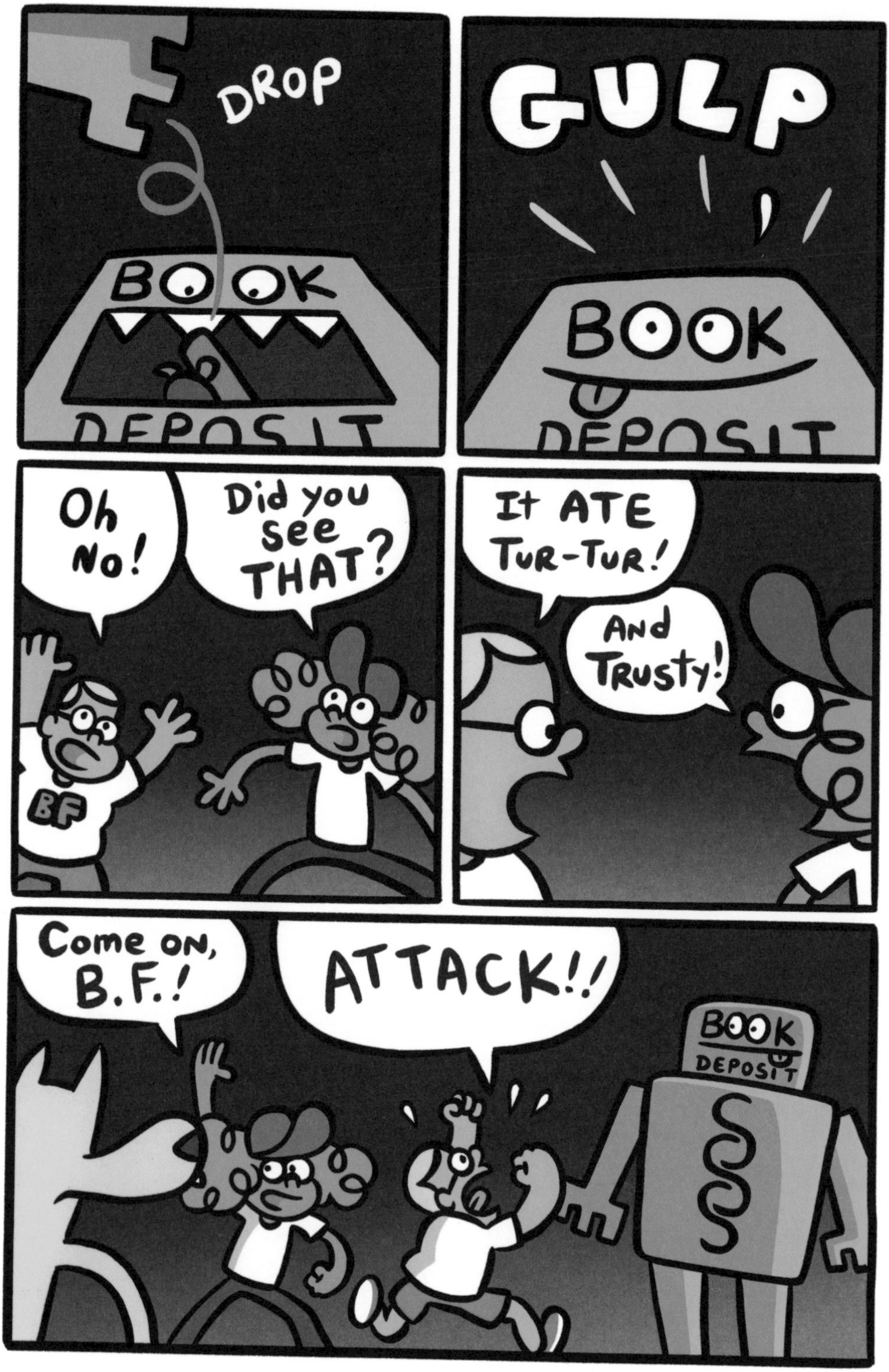
DROP
BOOK
DEPOSIT
GULP
BOOK
DEPOSIT
Oh No!
Did you see THAT?
BF
It ATE Tur-Tur!
And Trusty!
Come on, B.F.!
ATTACK!!
BOOK
DEPOSIT

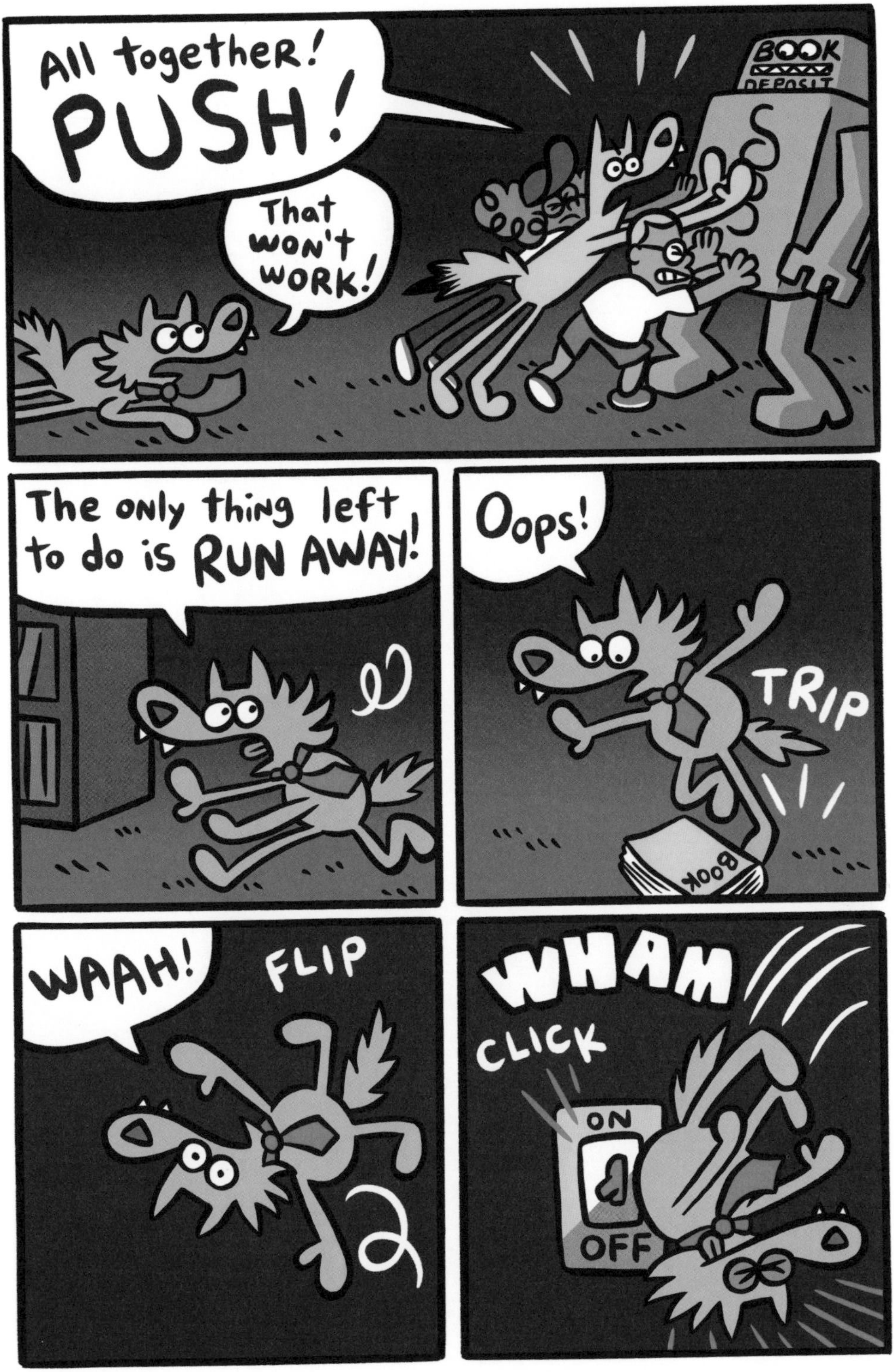
All together! PUSH!
That won't WORK!
BOOK DEPOSIT
The only thing left to do is RUN AWAY!
Oops!
TRIP
BOOK
WAAH!
FLIP
WHAM
CLICK
ON
OFF

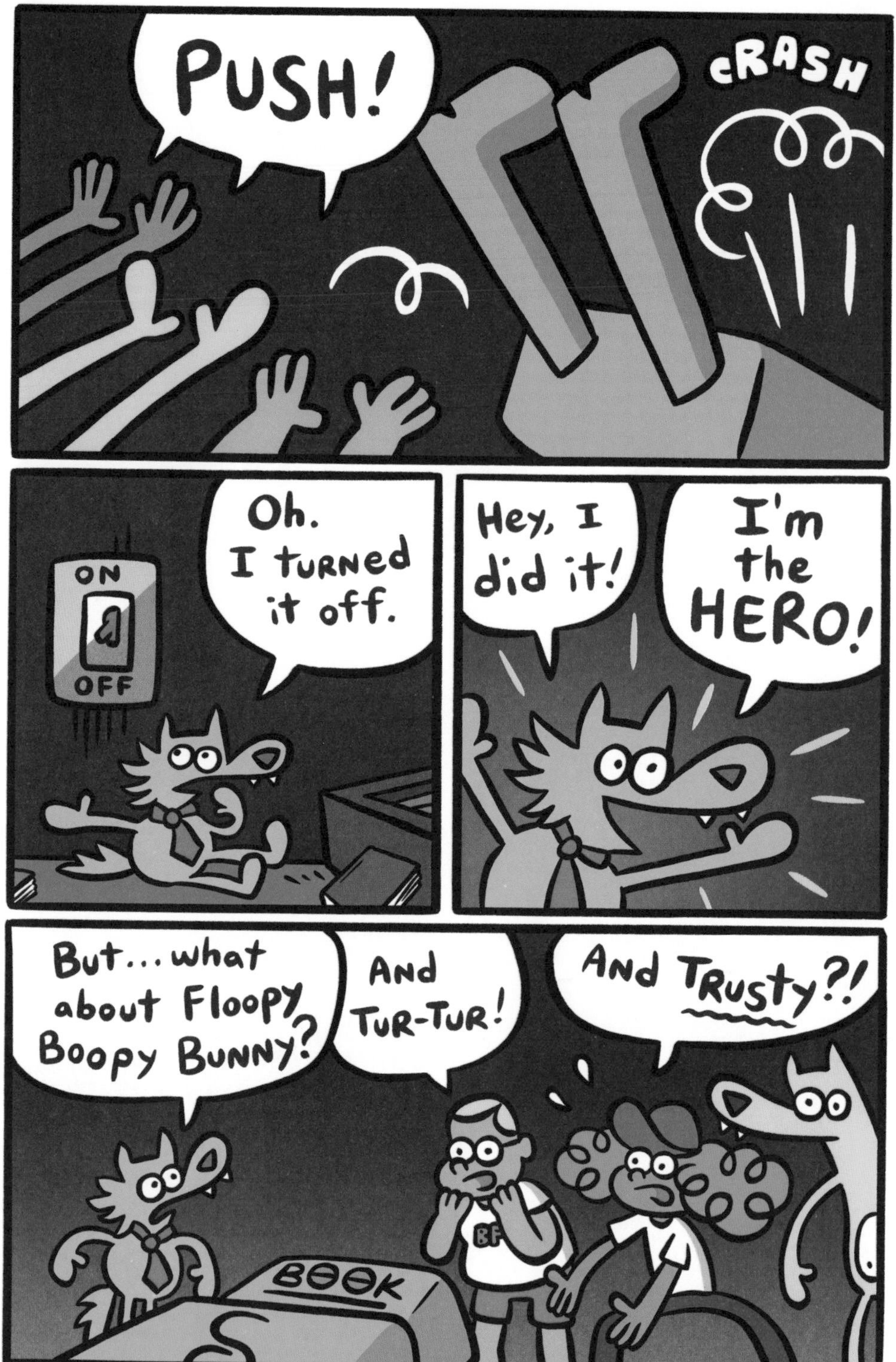
PUSH!
CRASH
Oh. I turned it off.
ON
OFF
Hey, I did it!
I'm the HERO!
But... what about Floopy Boopy Bunny?
AND TUR-TUR!
AND TRUSTY?!
BOOK
BF

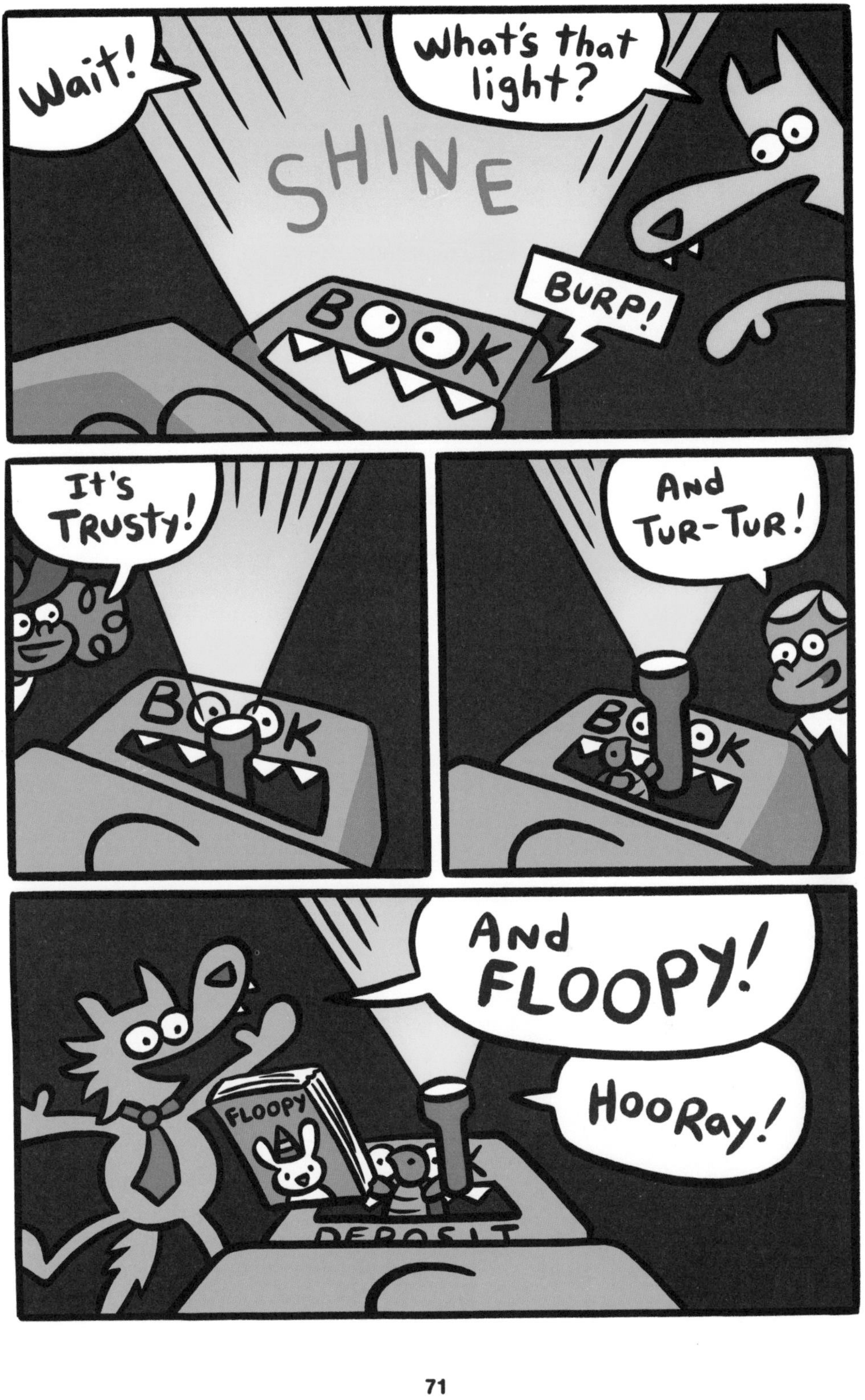
Wait!
What's that light?
SHINE
BOOK
BURP!
It's TRUSTY!
AND TUR-TUR!
AND FLOOPY!
FLOOPY
HOORAY!

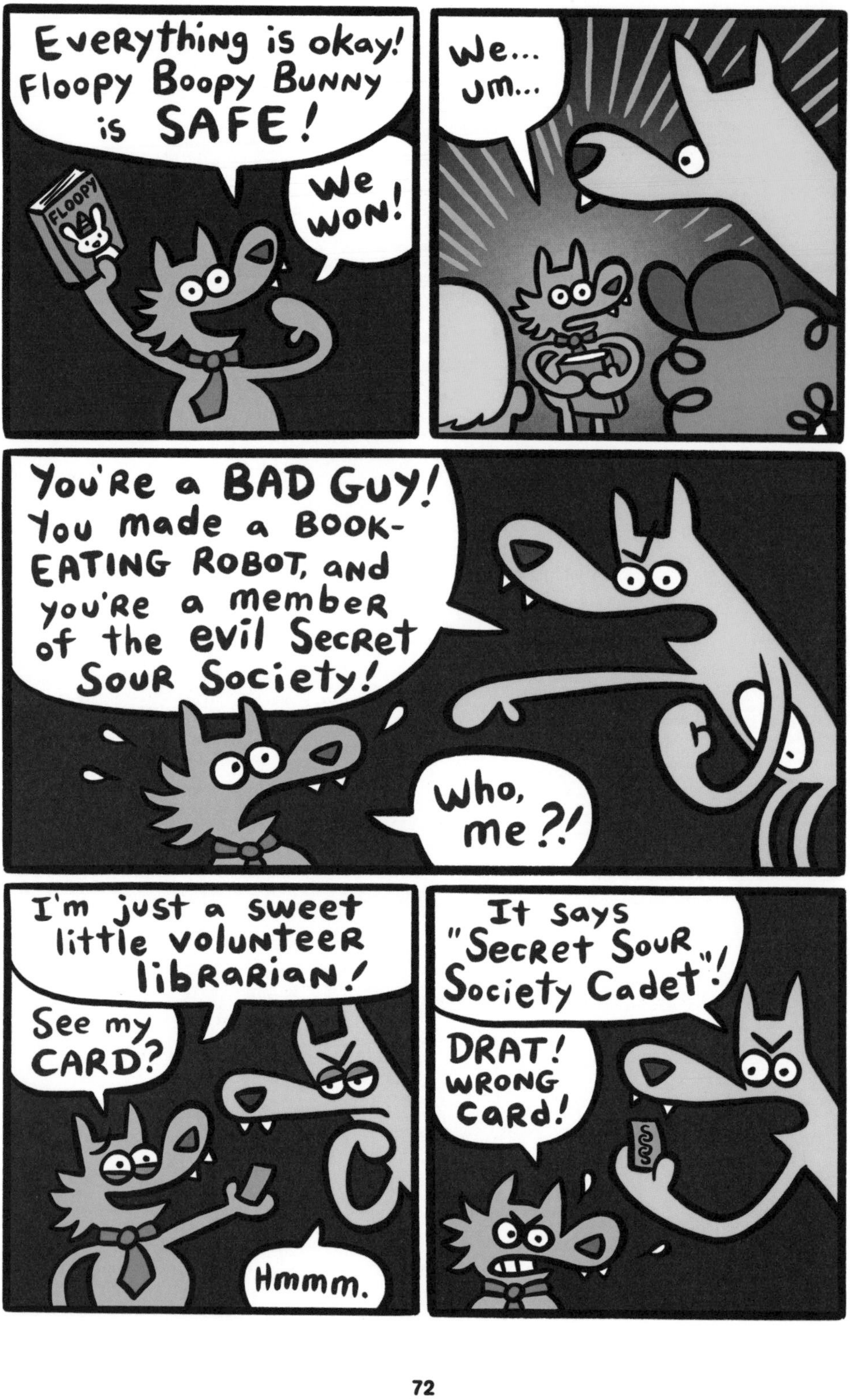
Everything is okay! Floopy Boopy Bunny is SAFE!
We WON!
FLOOPY
We... um...
You're a BAD GUY! You made a BOOK-EATING ROBOT, and you're a member of the evil Secret Sour Society!
Who, me?!
I'm just a sweet little volunteer librarian!
See my CARD?
Hmmm.
It says "Secret Sour Society Cadet"!
DRAT! WRONG card!

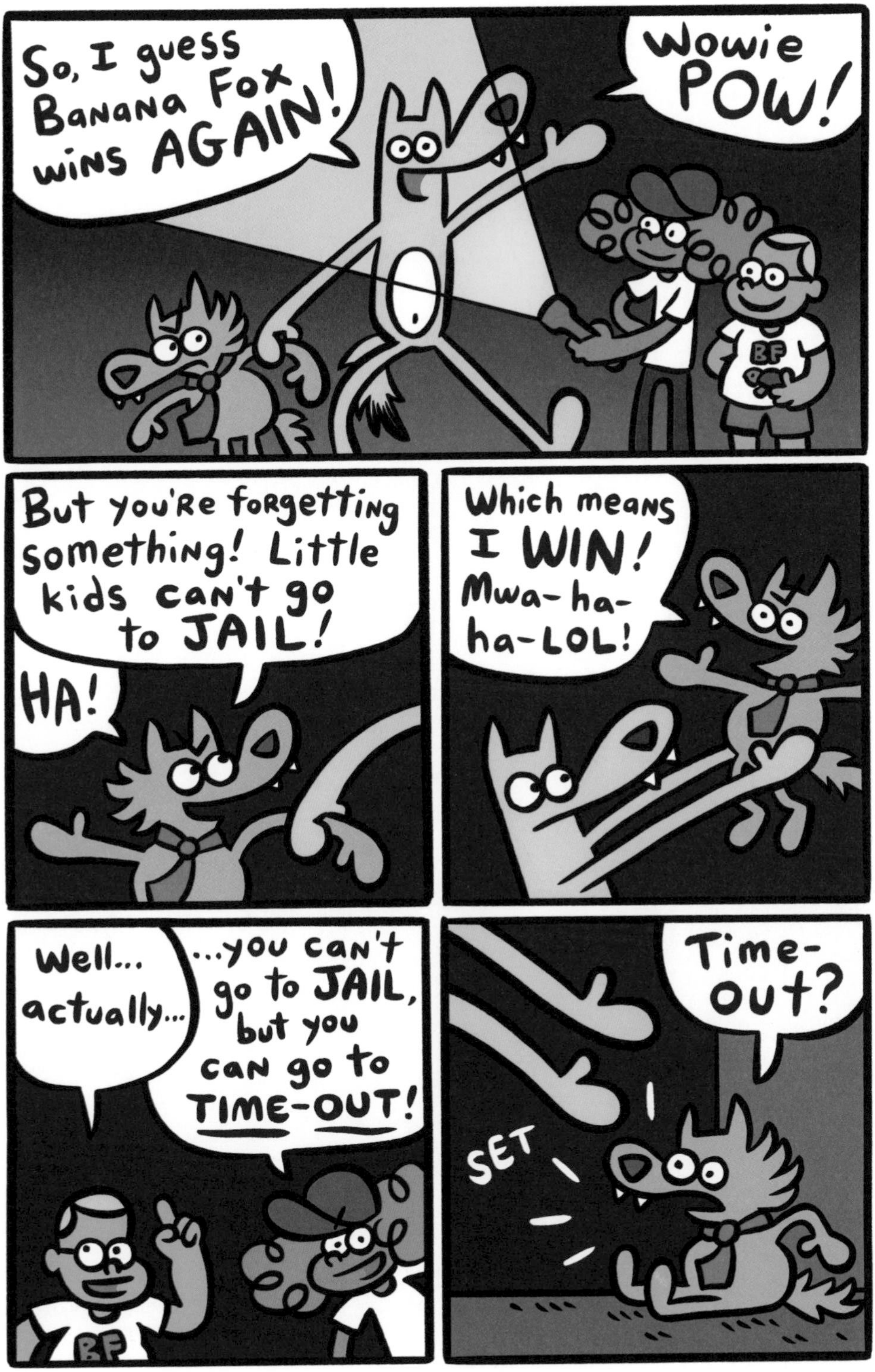
So, I guess Banana Fox wins AGAIN!
Wowie POW!
But you're forgetting something! Little kids can't go to JAIL!
HA!
Which means I WIN! Mwa-ha-ha-LOL!
Well... actually...
...you can't go to JAIL, but you can go to TIME-OUT!
Time-out?
SET
BF

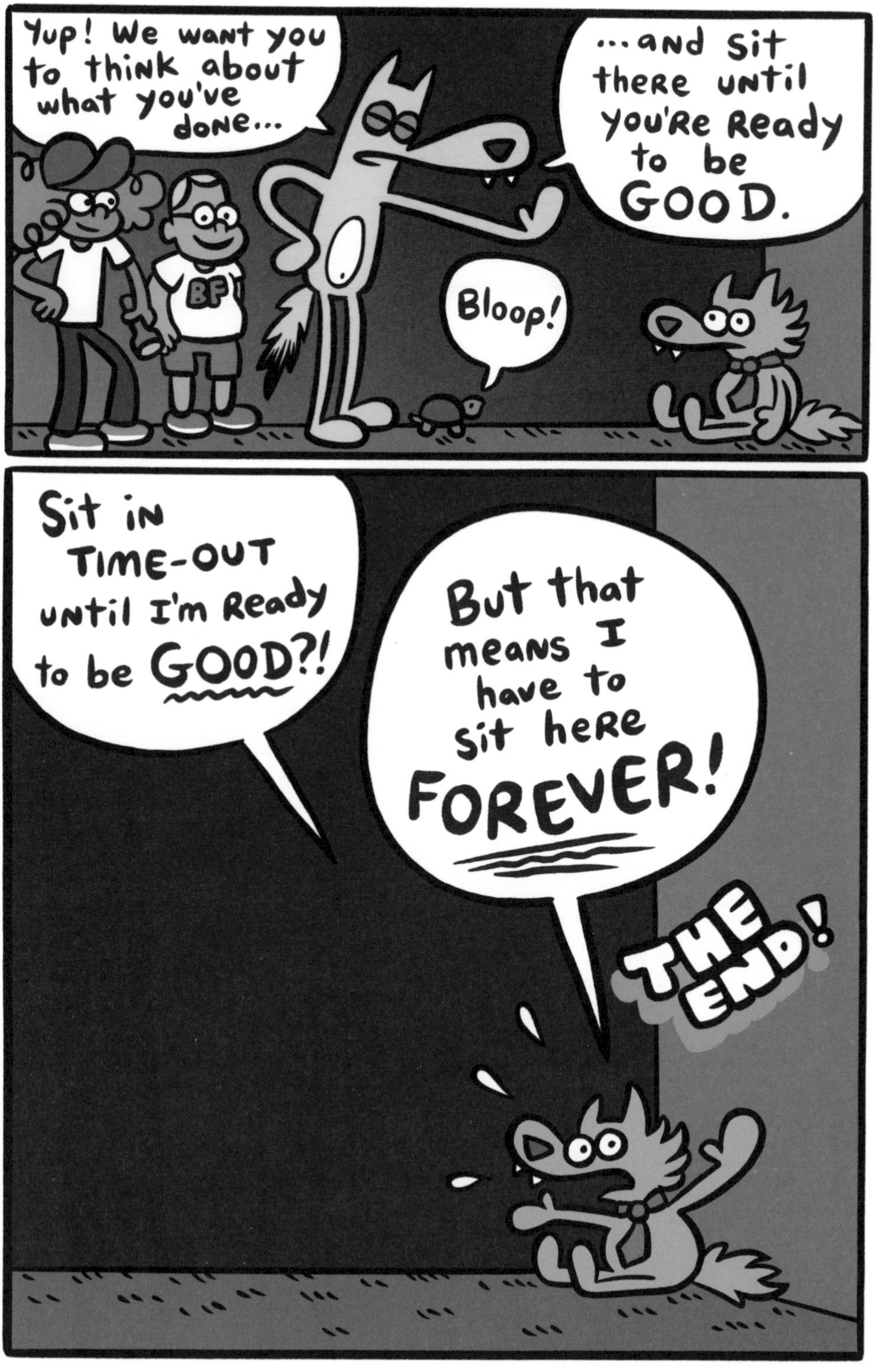

Yup! We want you to think about what you've done...
...and sit there until you're Ready to be GOOD.
Bloop!
Sit in TIME-OUT until I'm Ready to be GOOD?!
But that means I have to sit here FOREVER!
THE END!

JAMES KOCHALKA

is one of the most unique and prolific cartoonists working in America today. His comics have been published internationally, and he's developed animated cartoons for Nickelodeon. Among his best-known work is the Johnny Boo series, for which he won an Eisner Award in 2019. In 2011, James became the first official Vermont Cartoonist Laureate. He and his wife, Amy, continue to live in Vermont, where they raised their family of two boys and too many cats.